"*I want to be with you . . .*"

Anne rushed on, hearing the desperation creeping into her voice. "You don't have to love me back, Thady. As long as you care a little about me. And I'm not just a woman you need to use occasionally . . ."

"God, no! No!" He shook his head in anguished protest. "Don't say it was because of me. I tried. . . . I left before it went too far."

"What's too far, Thady?"

"Nothing happened between us."

"Too much happened. Too much that was unforgettable . . . to me."

"No!" His hand sliced the air as though he was warding off what she was pressing on him. "I can still hurt you, Anne. It's hard enough that I can't be . . . what you want me to be. . . ."

EMMA DARCY nearly became an actress until her fiancé declared he preferred to attend the theater *with* her. She became a wife and mother. Later, she took up oil painting—then architecture, designing the family home in New South Wales. Next came romance writing—"the hardest and most challenging of all the activities," she confesses. She now has more than forty bestselling romance novels to her credit, and regularly appears on Waldenbooks' Romance Bestsellers lists.

Books by Emma Darcy

HARLEQUIN PRESENTS
1511—DARK HERITAGE
1519—HEART OF THE OUTBACK
1536—AN IMPOSSIBLE DREAM
1555—THE UPSTAIRS LOVER
1570—NO RISKS, NO PRIZES
1579—A VERY STYLISH AFFAIR

EMMA DARCY

The Last Grand Passion

Harlequin Books

TORONTO • NEW YORK • LONDON
AMSTERDAM • PARIS • SYDNEY • HAMBURG
STOCKHOLM • ATHENS • TOKYO • MILAN
MADRID • WARSAW • BUDAPEST • AUCKLAND

Harlequin Presents Plus first edition October 1993
ISBN 0-373-11592-X

THE LAST GRAND PASSION

CHAPTER ONE

"DON'T YOU *WANT* TO GET married, Anne?"

Anne Tolliver cast an exasperated look at her youngest sister. Did *every* member of her family have to ask that question at *every* opportunity?

Jenny was not looking at her, nor at the sketches strewn across the desk. She was admiring her engagement ring, jiggling her fingers so that light sparkled off the facets of the diamond. It was all too obvious marriage was the only thing on Jenny's mind. Which was natural enough with her wedding barely four months away.

Anne's irritation melted into bleak loneliness as she remembered what she had been like at twenty-one. So madly in love...a head full of romantic dreams...all coming to nothing. Worse than nothing. It had been seven years since Thady Riordan had walked out of her life, but the memory of how she had felt with him still had the power to make any other man less than right for her.

Young as she was then, she had sensed the dark passions in his soul, the reaching out for something that she wanted to provide. Why he had chosen not to take what she had offered Anne still did not understand. It was well after he had returned to England that she began to understand there was far more to Thady Riordan than she had imagined.

When she had known him Thady had been a script writer, working on a joint British and Australian production for television, a mini series that was being partly shot at the studios where Anne worked as a wardrobe assistant. Barely a year after Thady had left her, his first play was a highly acclaimed hit on the London stage. It had been followed by others, two of which had been made into films.

His plays were stark and compelling revelations of human relationships. The depth and breadth of the knowledge behind them was both fascinating and disturbing. There were people comparing Thady Riordan to Tennessee Williams or Eugene O'Neill.

To Anne's mind, Thady stood alone. No other playwright exposed the folly and tragedy of human existence with such savagery and depth of feeling, laying bare the isolation and loneliness in every beating heart. Anne knew that inner loneliness only too well.

At least she had a career to keep her life busy and interesting. Her gaze drifted to the other end of her workroom. There on the bench along the wall sat the miniature stage sets she had built while experimenting with the production design for Thady Riordan's latest play.

So far it was her most prestigious job. The play had opened to great reviews two weeks ago, and the plaudits she received for her work should help to make her name in the theatrical world. Unfortunately that world was rather limited in Australia. She had to take work where and when she could get it, and it was scarce at the moment.

Which was just as well, she supposed, since she had promised to do the dresses for Jenny's wedding. She returned her attention to her sister, whose pretty vivacious face still wore a rapt expression. The diamond ring had caught a beam of sunlight from the window behind them.

"Jenny, I do need you to concentrate on all the details today if we're to get everything organised and made in good time," Anne gently reminded her.

"Sorry, Anne. I was just thinking...oh, never mind. What's next?"

"Are you happy with the jade silk taffeta for the bridesmaids?"

"Oh, yes! The girls are going to adore those dresses," Jenny enthused. "I don't know how you come up with such wonderful ideas."

"Costume design is my job," Anne stated dryly. "Among other things."

Jenny's face suddenly creased with uncertainty. "Anne, you don't mind not being one of my bridesmaids, do you?"

"Of course not."

"I felt awful about not asking you, but Mum said—" Her mouth twisted into a grimace as she pulled herself back from blurting out an embarrassing truth that could only hurt.

"It's all right," Anne hastily assured her.

She didn't have to wonder what her mother had said. She knew. "Three times a bridesmaid, never a bride." For Anne to fill that role again would undoubtedly tempt fate, since she had stood up for her other two younger sisters when they were married.

In fact Anne was relieved not to be involved in the wedding party. It would be enough to simply stand back and enjoy the whole production from a distance. Perhaps then she wouldn't be continually pestered with the question of when *she* was going to get married.

"It will be more fun for you to have your friends around you," she said, smiling to ease Jenny's concern.

Her sister heaved a big sigh. "I guess so. Though I still feel sorry that you won't be in my wedding photograph. Liz and Kate have you in theirs."

Both were framed for posterity and sitting in pride of place along the mantelpiece in her mother's living room. "I'm sure you'll look so beautiful that no-one will bother looking at anyone else," Anne assured the bride-to-be.

And after Jenny's photograph was added to the mantelpiece, their mother would undoubtedly use it as an even more pointed reminder that her oldest daughter was still on the shelf.

It could be argued that getting three out of four daughters married off was something of an achievement in these liberated times, but Anne doubted her mother would appreciate that argument. The women's liberation movement had passed Leonie Tolliver by. It was her entrenched opinion that a career, no matter how successful, was no substitute for marriage.

To Anne, a career was more fulfilling and rewarding than drifting along without any goals whatsoever, apart from waiting for a marriageable man to make her a housewife and mother. And if he then turned out to be the wrong man... Anne shuddered at the consequences.

"You didn't answer my question," Jenny remarked.

"What question?"

"About not wanting to get married."

"Don't you think I get enough of that question from Mum?" Anne demanded in a dry drawl.

It was meant to cut the subject dead, once and for all. But it didn't. Curiosity and concern gleamed in Jenny's bright brown eyes. "But what's going to happen to you if you never get married?"

"What *I* choose to happen," Anne said decisively.

"You must have been in love at least a couple of times, Anne," Jenny argued. "You *are* twenty-eight...."

"Which isn't exactly over the hill," Anne mocked.

Jenny flushed. "I didn't mean you were old. You've got a great figure and the kind of face that looks good even without make-up. Sexy hair..."

"*Sexy* hair?" Anne laughed, tugging at the untidy strands that had escaped from the loosely wound knot at the top of her head.

"Men like long hair. Especially when it's thick and soft and shiny and touchable like yours."

"You obviously have expert knowledge," Anne teased, reaching over to stroke Jenny's blonde bob.

Jenny sighed her exasperation. "I'm serious, Anne. There must have been guys attracted to you over the years."

"I wasn't attracted to them," she replied lightly.

"What about Tom Colby?"

Anne felt her face tightening. She could never think of that dreadful self-delusion without pain. If Tom had not looked like Thady, if she had not felt so lonely... But neither of those excuses lessened her guilt where Tom was concerned.

"I wasn't in love with him," she stated flatly.

"Then why did you have an affair with him?"

"Because I was curious and I thought I was in love." She forced a dismissive smile. "Maybe I'm not as lucky as you, Jenny. It didn't work out."

The big brown eyes softened with compassion. "Were you terribly hurt, Anne?"

"I'd really prefer not to talk about it."

"You shouldn't let it sour you off all men."

"It doesn't. I wish you and your Brian every happiness in the world," she said with fervent sincerity.

"I want you to be happy, too," came the equally fervent response. "What would you consider the right man for you, Anne?"

The telephone rang.

Anne was grateful for the interruption. This personal probing by her sister had gone far enough. She was reaching for the receiver when Jenny suddenly jumped to her feet in a flutter.

"It'll probably be Brian wanting to know if everything is okay," she babbled as she skipped around the desk. "In fact, I'm certain it's Brian."

Anne withdrew her outstretched hand, allowing Jenny to snatch up the receiver.

"Oh, Brian!" she gushed. "I'm so glad you called. The bridesmaids' dresses are fabulous. We're just about to start on—" She stopped.

Anne looked up in idle interest, wondering what amazing piece of news Brian was relating to distract Jenny from her present obsession.

Jenny's face was flushed with embarrassment. "Oh, I'm sorry. Wrong person," she gabbled, then gave a nervous little laugh as she cupped her hand over the receiver and looked at Anne. "It's for you."

"Who is it?"

"It's a bad line. I don't know. I think it's Roy somebody or somebody Roy."

Anne didn't know anybody of that name. Maybe someone with a job proposal.

"Annelise Tolliver." It was her full name, her professional name.

"It's Thady, Anne. Thady Riordan."

The soft Irish lilt sent prickles down Anne's spine. Her heart stopped dead. Her head whirled with incredulity and doubts, yet there was no mistaking that voice, and not even seven years had dimmed its effect on her.

Seven years!

And not one word from him since he had walked away from her and pursued his own purpose on the other side of the world.

Why had he remembered her now? What possible purpose could he have in calling, speaking to her as though the long separation had never been?

"Anne? Am I calling at an inconvenient time?"

Her eyes focused on the clock. Eleven twenty-four. She wondered what time it was in London. Her mind was incapable of calculating the difference. Nine...ten hours. Backwards or forwards? It didn't matter anyway. She tried to compose herself. Somehow she made her tongue work.

"The time is fine. You surprised me. A call from you is hardly a daily occurrence, Thady."

"Anne, I saw the play last night," he said quietly. "I saw what you had done with it."

What *she* had done!

For a moment her head pounded dizzily as the meaning of what he was telling her hammered through her mind. Thady couldn't be calling from England. Not if he had seen *her* work on his play. He had to be in Australia, right here in Sydney! The distance between them suddenly dwindled into nothing.

Into the dead silence Thady's voice spoke again, soft, intimate, promising. "I'm in Sydney, Anne. I want to see you."

His words triggered a turmoil of hopes, fears and wild desires. Anne tried to steady herself, to be sensible. Thady hadn't called her *before* he saw the play. His interest in seeing her had been prompted by her work. She would be an absolute fool to think it could be anything else.

"I'd like that, Thady," she said, trying her utmost to sound as calm and collected as a professional person should in such circumstances. Yet a deeply primitive need for his approval prompted her to ask, "Did my production design fit your vision of the play?"

"More so than I could ever have imagined, Anne," he said with the caressing warmth that used to curl her toes. It still did. "I can't stop thinking about it. I want to see you, talk to you about it. Can you meet me for lunch?"

She was supposed to be spending the day with Jenny, going through the sketches, finalising details. But surely Jenny would understand how important this was to her. She could say it was important business. Vitally important. Which it was.

"Or dinner tonight?" Thady pressed.

No, she thought wildly. She couldn't bear to lose one minute of being with him. He might be flying back to England tomorrow. Anything might happen to prevent their meeting between now and tonight. She couldn't, wouldn't risk postponing the time.

"I can make it to lunch," she said decisively.

Jenny started waving her hands and pulling faces at her, but Thady was on the line, talking to her, and nothing else mattered.

"I'm at the Park Hyatt. Right next to the harbour bridge. Could you join me here? Or if you'd like to suggest somewhere else . . ."

"No. That's fine."

"What time suits you?"

She needed time to get ready, time to get there. "One o'clock?"

"One o'clock," he confirmed. "I'll look forward to it, Anne. Thank you."

That was it. An invitation and an acceptance. No "How are you?" No "What have you been doing all these years?" But there would be time for that when they met, Anne argued to herself. Or did he only care about what she had done for his play?

Seven years and no word from him. Seven years, during which he had been publicly connected to several beautiful women. Anne had seen photographs in the celebrity sections of women's magazines. Thady Riordan with Lady So-and-so, successful young playwright being lionised by London society. Thady Riordan with leading actress. Thady Riordan with scintillating socialite. But he hadn't married any of them, Anne fiercely reminded herself.

"What's the matter with you, Anne?"

Jenny's sharp tone and question snapped her attention to her sister. "Nothing," she mumbled. The wall clock read eleven twenty-seven. Three minutes for the world to turn.

"You make an appointment for lunch when we're supposed to be spending the day together," Jenny reminded her. "Then you sit there with glazed eyes. You're still holding the phone, you know. So what's going on?"

The mixture of accusation and concern brought a wry smile to Anne's lips. "Sorry, Jenny. I guess I was in shock. That was Thady Riordan on the phone."

Jenny's eyes widened. "You mean the guy who wrote the play you just did?"

"The same. He's over here from England and he wants to meet me. It's a professional opportunity I can't miss, Jenny."

"Wow! Go for it, Anne! We can do this stuff tomorrow." Her eyes glittered with excitement at the idea of her sister meeting an international celebrity. "From the photos I've seen of him he's a gorgeous hunk. What are you going to wear?"

"I don't know. I need to be alone to think about this, Jenny. Do you mind?"

"No, that's okay! I'll hop off now. I hope it works out great for you, Anne."

"Thanks, Jenny. Come around tomorrow and we'll finish working on these sketches."

"Sure!" She was already on her way out when a last thought struck her. "Wear your hair down, Anne. It's sexy."

Sexy!

It hadn't been sexy seven years ago, Anne thought with grim irony. Not sexy enough to draw Thady into any more than a few gentle kisses. What had he felt for her then? He had to have been attracted to her. Had he thought she was too young for him? Too young and inexperienced for any deep involvement?

Well, she wasn't so young and inexperienced now, Anne thought as she headed for her bathroom. This was a chance to find out the answers to all the questions that had haunted her over the years, a chance to settle what she felt about Thady Riordan once and for all.

Was it the dream of a young heart?

Or was it a passion that would never die?

Anne was aware of her pulse quickening as she tossed off her clothes. Stay calm, she told herself fiercely. Having showered, dressed, and groomed to her professional best, Anne surveyed her appearance with critical eyes, trying to assess what Thady would see.

The cream linen suit skimmed the curves of her figure with enough style to be feminine without being overtly sexy. Her stockings matched the taupe silk blouse, very much the in-fashion colour at the moment. Her cream high heels and handbag featured a touch of gold, which her gold ear studs and the fine gold chains around her neck picked up.

She had brushed her long, thick, honey-coloured hair into a soft dip above one ear before looping it into a loosely wound knot at the top of her head. It was an elegant, sophisticated style that accentuated her long, graceful neck. The make-up she had applied lent a light sheen to her smooth skin, subtly highlighted her darkly lashed amber eyes and outlined the full feminine curve of her lips.

She looked good.

She didn't look twenty-one any more.

Thady Riordan wanted to see the woman she was now. Anne had come a long way from the tumble-haired, scattily dressed wardrobe assistant who had briefly caught his attention. Anne knew there was no going back to that young woman with her head full of dreams. The mirror reflected an experienced, confident woman.

Thady Riordan was about to meet Annelise Tolliver.

CHAPTER TWO

THE TAXI RIDE from her home at Paddington to the Park Hyatt at Campbell's Cove took a bare twenty minutes. Anne needed every second of it to settle her composure. It was precisely one o'clock as she stepped out of the cab.

The roar of a train crossing the harbour bridge startled her, and the doorman quickly ushered her into the hotel which was completely sound-proofed. The sudden quiet emphasised the elegance of the decor.

An expanse of highly polished tiled floor swept to a magnificent view of the opera house through the long windows on the other side of the room. Wonderful floral arrangements graced tall vases and urns, forming splashes of exotic luxury. The reception desk was a period piece, its simplicity statement enough no bustle occurred in this hotel.

Unobtrusively a number of staff in smart black suits waited patiently to give any service or courtesy. Anne wondered if she should notify the receptionist of her arrival, but even as she considered it, her eye caught movement from the seating area to the right of the entrance.

She turned her head and there he was, the man who had held her heart captive from their first meeting so many years ago. He was already on his feet and moving steadily, resolutely towards her.

Their eyes locked, simmering green and golden amber. Anne breathed in deeply to counteract the sudden surge of excitement that was almost panic. Her heart seemed to be beating much faster, creating a drumming effect in her ears. Her mind instructed her to move forward to greet him, but her feet didn't receive the message. They stood riveted to the floor as her eyes absorbed the physical presence of Thady Riordan.

Recognition had been instant, yet he was different from her memory of him, different from her dreams of him. Disturbingly different. She tried to pinpoint what it was, because she felt the difference coming from him, causing her to react physically in a way she never had.

Her skin was prickling, tightening, all over her body. She was acutely aware of her femininity, the silk of her blouse skimming the soft swell of her breasts, the close fit of her skirt around her hips, the bareness of her thighs above her stockings.

Something had changed. But what?

His physique looked the same. He was well over medium height but not overly tall. The grey suit he wore displayed the strong breadth of his shoulders and the muscularity of his thighs. Perhaps there was an added hardness to his face, a hollowness in his cheeks that threw his bone structure into gaunt relief.

It was a strongly chiselled face with a high, wide forehead, angular jaw line, prominent nose and clean-cut chin. The contrast of soft hair, a riot of black curls flopping across his forehead and tumbling over his ears and collar, gave him an untamed look that was compellingly attractive.

Was it his eyes that were different? She remembered them as dark fathomless green eyes, deeply set and shadowed by thick black lashes. Eyes filled with gentle humour when he smiled. He was smiling now, a whimsical little smile that accentuated the sensuality of his wide, full-lipped mouth, a mouth that Anne knew could weave magical feelings inside her.

There was something more powerful, more dominant about the way he walked towards her. Ready to take and do whatever he willed. Did success engender that in people? Did wealth? It was in his eyes. No trace of gentleness. They were hard and determined. Perhaps even . . . yes, ruthless.

A convulsive shiver ran down Anne's spine. What did he want of her? Her mind reasoned that he couldn't take anything unless she let him, but her body was registering a terrible vulnerability to this man, whatever he had become.

He was more handsome than any memory or photograph could ever capture and retain. As he came to a halt in front her, Anne noticed the fine quality of his suit, his white silk shirt and silk designer tie, the obvious trappings of success. She had looked past the clothes to see the man, but logic argued that the clothes were now part of the man, a part she had never known.

"You remember me?" he asked in a voice that was barely audible.

Anne jerked her gaze up from the brilliantly coloured tie. She remonstrated with herself to pull herself together and be a bit professional. Her imagination was running riot.

"Thady," she acknowledged in a fair semblance of a matter-of-fact tone.

"You've grown more beautiful, Anne."

His eyes said desirable. Intensely and immediately desirable.

"You've grown more handsome," she replied, the words tripping off her tongue without any sensible thought at all.

His smile took on an ironic curl. "You never married."

"No. It seems we're two of a kind."

There was a quick flitter of expressions, speculation, relief, then a settling into satisfaction. "That was what I thought last night," he said softly. "Someone in tune with me. It was an exciting revelation to see how well you understood what I'd written, Anne. To know we share the same passions."

He paused, then added almost carelessly, "There's no-one you're attached to at the present moment?"

Resentment washed through Anne, sobering her stupidly infatuated response to him. After all these years, and after what he had done and hadn't done, did he really think he could walk back into her life, just like that?

She had never fully admitted to herself how deeply in love she had been with Thady Riordan. But this was not the man she had loved. Not even remotely. That Thady had made her feel like Cinderella every time she had gone out with him. As though she were beautiful and precious and very special to him. This Thady was making her feel like . . . Whatever it was, it was deeply disturbing.

"As it happens, I'm not attached to anyone at present," she stated coolly. "But I didn't come here to discuss my private life, Thady. I thought you wanted to talk about my work on your play."

He raised a challenging eyebrow. "You think our work doesn't reflect our private lives, Anne?"

"Not all of it!"

"That's why I want to know all that's happened to you. How you've come to where you are now."

Smooth as silk he was, primed to pounce whichever way she moved. The aura of kindness and giving he had once worn was totally gone.

"I doubt we could fit in seven years of my life over lunch," she said with a touch of bitterness.

"The time it takes means nothing to me."

That was a lie. It *had* to be a lie. "What brought you back to Australia, Thady?" she tossed at him.

"Memories," he said in the soft Irish lilt that played havoc with her nervous system.

Anne steeled herself against this further lie. If he had a treasure chest of memories of her, it had taken a hell of a long time for him to open it!

"There were no memories worth keeping," she asserted, rejecting the idea that what they had once shared meant anything to her. "At least there were none for me," she added to completely smash that insultingly facile approach from him.

A bittersweet smile curved his lips. He lifted a hand to her face. A feather-light touch stroked down her cheek, her throat, shoulder, arm. "Then perhaps we can make new memories, Anne. Ones you won't want to dismiss so easily."

All the reasonable logic in Anne's mind flew into chaos, her emotions twisting into utter turmoil. She had not expected such directness. For whatever reason, Thady Riordan had decided he wanted her, and he could have her.

His fingers closed around her arm, pressing a seductive possessiveness. Heat radiated from his touch, infiltrating her entire body. Her stomach contracted in a clutch of sheer physical desire. Thady Riordan had lived in her mind for so long. And she *could* have him now if she wanted.

What would it be like to know all she had never had with him? To have the kind of intimacy she had craved? To lie in his arms and make love? But was this man capable of love?

He was not the Thady she remembered. He was more the man who had written the plays. Dark and dangerous, emanating a frightening flow of hidden undercurrents.

"What do you want from me, Thady?" she blurted, desperately wishing she could read his mind.

"Nothing you can't freely give, Anne."

"What does that mean?" Her eyes sharply challenged his claim.

Determination glittered back. "What do you want most in the world, Anne?"

It had been *him* up until a few moments ago.

Anne decided to let him think that ambition was her highest priority. She lifted her chin in defiance. "The most important thing in the world to me is my career."

It jolted him. His hand slid away from her arm. The flesh on his face seemed to tighten. His lips thinned. The warmth in the green eyes glittered into a chilling cynicism.

"Then I'll give you that," he said, still undeterred from having whatever he thought she could give him.

That jolted Anne. Of course it was possible with his connections and influence to open paths for her that she could never forge herself, but to use that power to cold-bloodedly bribe her into his bed was the last action she would ever have expected from him.

"Why, Thady? What's in it for you?" she asked, inwardly pleading for some understanding of why he was treating her like this. "What do you get out of it?"

His eyes emptied of all expression. "I've arranged for lunch to be served in my suite. Shall we go there and discuss the matter?"

The thought of being alone with him in his suite sent a quiver of fear through Anne. So many emotions warred through her that she knew intuitively that such a move could only bring her grief.

Yet pride insisted that she appear totally unmoved by this arrangement. Pride insisted that she see this encounter with Thady Riordan through to its absolute end, whatever that entailed. Only then might she be able to cut herself free of all the years of yearning for what might have been.

"And after lunch, Thady...what happens then?" Her eyes derided his obvious purpose for getting her alone with him.

"Why, Anne," he drawled lightly, "what happens after lunch is entirely up to you."

A mocking little smile lingered on his lips as he linked her arm to his and drew her towards the elevator. She didn't resist. Although she felt sickened to her soul, she could not tear herself free of him. Not yet. Perhaps not ever.

Anne had the miserable feeling that they had both lost what they had most wanted. Yet they were both tied to whatever happened next.

CHAPTER THREE

ANNE'S LEGS WERE trembling by the time they reached
the door to his suite. When Thady withdrew the support of his arm to open the door, a sudden pause in her
heartbeat made her sway. It lasted only an instant before she managed to recover herself, yet when Thady
turned to usher her inside, something about her caused
him to hesitate.

Whether she looked pale or feverish, Anne had no
idea. There was a flicker of pain or regret in his eyes,
perhaps the memory of a different time, a different
place, a different person. It was gone so quickly Anne
wasn't sure she saw it. His face reflected set determination for the here and now.

"Be my guest," he said as he gestured for Anne to
enter ahead of him.

"As long as that's all I am," she returned with
pointed irony, then pushed her legs forward and past
him with as much dignity as she could muster.

It was a spacious, plush apartment. The walls were
angled in such a way that they made niched areas for
the dining setting, a lounge suite and a king-size bed
with all of its convenient facilities. Floor-to-ceiling
glass gave a spectacular view of the harbour, and the
curtains were pulled back to make a point of it.

She heard the door close and kept on walking towards the view. "You do yourself proud these days, Thady," she remarked, feeling absurdly conscious of the bed and even more conscious of his eyes following her.

"I can afford it now."

"Do you favour water views?" she prattled on, words spilling out to break her tense awareness of his physical presence behind her.

"Yes."

"Different from the old days when we slummed it together, isn't it?"

"Yes. It's different."

"Do you enjoy it more?" she quietly asked.

As stupidly impossible as it was, she yearned for him to say that nothing was more enjoyable than the time they had shared, the simple fun they'd had, the walks and talks and the easy laughter between them.

He made no reply. His silence chewed up Anne's memories as effectively as a kitchen disposal unit. She stared out at the water, deriding herself for asking the question in the first place. Wasn't wealth always better than poverty?

She heard the rattle of ice, the popping of a cork, the fizz of champagne as it was poured into glasses. The fizz of success, she thought sourly, which he had shared with other women.

He came to stand beside her, handed her a glass of champagne. He lifted his in a toast. "To Annelise Tolliver and her career."

She forced herself to look up at him with a bland smile. "Thank you, Thady." Then, unable to contain her seething bitterness, she added, "Do you make good on your promises? Or are they as false as your interest in me once was?"

His eyes seemed to go flat, opaque. "I was interested, Anne."

"You left without saying goodbye."

"If we'd met again we would have become lovers," he stated as a matter of fact.

"Was that so bad?"

"Yes," he replied simply. "Yes, at that time it would have been bad."

"But it's not so bad to become lovers now."

"That's correct. It's not so bad now."

"How very reassuring," she drawled, hating him for his decisions. No consultation. No discussion. Only what he wanted. She raised her glass in a toast to him. "To good and bad," she said with brittle mockery. "May the bad sometimes win."

They both sipped the champagne. Anne had to fight against choking on hers. She wished she hadn't brought up the past. She couldn't deny she would have been his lover for the taking at almost any time they'd been together. The mutual acknowledgement shamed her.

She could feel Thady brooding, looking intently at her. He exuded a magnetism that her body responded to whether she liked it or not. Every breath she took seemed full of him, as though the air itself was permeated with the powerful pull of his physical presence.

"Do you ever feel lonely with your career, Anne?" he asked softly. "Don't you want more than that?"

He knew where to strike. Where to twist the knife. But the same knife was in her hands. She lifted her eyes and hurled her knowledge at him.

"Everyone suffers moments of loneliness at times, Thady, with or without a career. Isn't that what you write in your plays? Utter and total loneliness? Loneliness so extreme that no person should ever experience it."

His fingers were on her lips, silencing her, in a motion so swift that it caught Anne by surprise. His eyes had turned to a greenish-black. His brow furrowed. Anne sensed that what she'd said was some unacceptable violation of his private world.

Just as suddenly his mood changed. His eyes gathered a lighter gleam that mocked her attempt at hurting him. He lifted his hand away, palm out in a gesture implying he had nothing to hide.

"That's why I'm always alone," he said matter-of-factly. "I write what I know. I write what I feel. I know loneliness best. That is my life, Anne. My constant companion."

"Not exactly *constant*," she flashed at him, remembering her heartache over the glamorous women who had starred in his life. "Your affairs with various *companions* have fed the gossip columns around the world."

One eyebrow rose in derisive challenge. "Do you believe everything you read?"

"Are you denying that you've been attached to an array of beautiful women?"

"There was no affair. Not in the sense you mean."

"What was there, then?"

"Publicity."

"You don't expect me to believe that?" Anne scoffed.

He shrugged. "Believe what you please."

"Sure! You live like a monk in a monastery."

"When I want to."

"And all those highly desirable women were left disappointed."

"They meant nothing to me."

"You remained totally celibate?" She couldn't believe it. Not from the kind of man he was showing her today.

"I'm a man with normal urges," he bit out.

"So you did—"

"Yes, I did," he snapped. A dark torment suddenly swirled from his eyes. "But only after you took up with Tom Colby."

Anne's jealous anger froze into shock. The mad triumph of having forced Thady into his admission was completely shattered. Had she lost Thady because of Tom? But how could that be? It didn't make any sense.

"What do you know about Tom?" she cried in anguish.

"Enough to know I want what *he* had."

CHAPTER FOUR

ANNE COULD FEEL the blood draining from her face. Shock upon shock trembled through her. Thady knew about her relationship with Tom Colby. He hadn't touched any other woman until after he knew. Or so he said. And the vehement possessiveness in his voice just now . . . wanting what she had given Tom . . .

Thady could have had that and more if he hadn't left her. She had loved *him*. Only him. And she hadn't met Tom Colby until three years after Thady had gone from her life. And then she had deceived herself into believing Tom was just like Thady.

She lifted pained eyes to the man who had twice led her into a deep personal hell. "If you wanted me, why didn't you come back?"

His mouth twisted. His eyes simmered with soft mockery. "I couldn't belong in your dreams, Anne."

"What dreams?"

"Getting married, having children, the happy ever after. When I heard about Tom Colby, I hoped he'd give you everything you wanted."

"How altruistic of you, Thady. Caring so much about my needs. Playing God on my behalf."

He flinched.

Anne drove on savagely, wanting to hurt as he had hurt her by arrogantly judging that he knew best for both of them. "Did it make you feel less of a failure when you thought my dreams were being answered?"

"A failure?" He gave a harsh, derisive laugh. "Because I don't fit into the nice neat slot that you consider acceptable?" His bitter amusement faded into a grim smile as he quoted from *Hamlet*. "There are more things in heaven and earth, Anne, than are dreamt of in your philosophy."

"And *you* know all about them," she taunted, smarting at his condescension.

"Enough not to wish them on anyone else." His eyes bored into hers with certain knowledge. "But you're learning about the downside of life, aren't you, Anne? You're learning about loneliness, aren't you? Your work on my play was not all skilful artistry. You *knew* what it was about. You created from what you *knew*. Was Tom Colby responsible for that?"

You were the one responsible, she wanted to say, but she bit the words back. He would never appreciate how much she had felt for him, how deep it had gone. Yet she must have touched something in him for there to have been no interest in any other woman until he knew she had been taken.

Perhaps it was because he hadn't had sex with her, the fruit he had forbidden himself, the sweet young dreamer he'd turned his back on out of some core of decency.

"How did you hear about Tom?" she asked.

"From Alex Korbett."

Alex, her boss at the time. Anne had learnt a lot about production design under Alex's tutoring. She remembered his trip to England. He hadn't mentioned seeing Thady Riordan. There was no reason he should. He had been full of talk about what was being done in the theatres over there, which was their common interest.

No doubt his meeting with Thady had been totally incidental. There would have been a chat about mutual acquaintances in Australia. Alex loved to gossip about people. As soon as her name had come up he would have prattled away about her involvement with Tom.

"Did you love him, Anne?"

She stared hopelessly into his eyes.

"I answered your questions," he reminded her softly.

She dragged out the truth. A truth of which she was ashamed, but the truth nevertheless. "No. I didn't love him."

"But you gave yourself to him."

"Completely."

That was the truth, too, as far as it went. She supposed Thady considered that it gave him free licence to go after a loveless affair with her since she had done what she had done. After all, here she was, still unmarried, a self-declared career woman who owned to no other dreams.

"Was it out of loneliness?" he asked.

Out of need, she thought despairingly. The need to be loved. The need to be loved as she had imagined

Thady would have loved her. But she couldn't tell him that. It was even more shaming, and far too revealing. He didn't love her. He only wanted her. Free and clear of dreams.

"Perhaps I have the normal urges of a woman, Thady," she answered dryly.

Satisfaction gleamed in his eyes. "In that case," he said easily, "we're equals."

He lifted a hand and gently laid his fingertips on her cheek. She felt the skin beneath his touch burn, felt a quiver of weakness run through the muscles of her legs, felt her heart leap into chaotic pounding. Half of her wanted to back away, but the other half wavered on a knife-edge of curiosity and anticipation. The pull was still there, no matter what had been said or done.

Not for one moment did his eyes move from hers, mesmerising in their relentless purpose as he trailed his fingers over the smooth curve of her cheek, along her jaw line, down her throat to the gold chains, which he slowly traced around to the nape of her neck.

"You feel the same way I do, Anne," he murmured, his voice husky with desire. "The wanting each other never died, did it? The moment I looked at you, you looked at me, I knew it was still there for us."

Did it all come down to this? she agonised in silent torment. All the pain, the grief, the loneliness, the wanting? Just two bodies coming together to satisfy an animal instinct?

Her stomach churned between excitement and revulsion. The knowing caress of the erotic spots around the nape of her neck was almost hypnotic. Cats purred for this, she thought, feeling a thrum of sensation spreading through her nerve ends.

Thady's fingers drifted up to the pins that secured her hair. "Your hair is so beautiful. Far too beautiful to be pinned away."

It was what Tom used to say. Tom, who had believed he loved her, at least for a time. But there was no love coming from the man who was touching her, arousing responses in her, wanting her to give what she had given Tom in his place.

A sense of terrible betrayal ripped through Anne. She twisted away from Thady's seductive touch, out of his reach, barely aware of what she was doing, where she was going. She felt sick to her very soul at all the deceptions that were played for the appeasement of physical desire.

Her eyes fell on the bed. She walked towards it, gripped by a wild urge to wreak vengeance on the man who had reduced her love to sex.

Every person destroys best the thing they love the most, she thought savagely, and the feelings Thady had aroused in her made Anne hell-bent on destruction. He shouldn't be able to do that to her. It wasn't fair. It wasn't right. The power he still had over her needed to be smashed once and for all.

He wouldn't be ending it this time. She would. Once and for all. She'd reduce everything she'd ever felt for him to dead ashes so there could be no possible comeback from him. Ever again!

Memories! She would give him memories. Memories he'd carry with him for the rest of his life. The innocent dreamer had come of age, all right! She had no illusions left at all.

Anne set her handbag and the glass of champagne on the bedside table and wheeled around to face him, her eyes burning with fiery contempt.

"You don't have to dress it up, Thady. You don't have to play pretend. You want me? You can have me. At no cost to yourself. You can save your pretty compliments for other women."

She struck a provocative, flaunting pose as she took off her suit coat and dropped it on the floor. "Come and get it, Thady," she invited silkily. "Take what you want. Have what Tom had."

The stunned look on his face gave her a fierce but grim satisfaction.

"Do you have a thing about hair, Thady?" she taunted, reaching up to remove her hairpins. "Does it excite you in some special way?"

His face tightened as though she had hit him. Two red slashes appeared high on his cheekbones. Violent anger, no doubt, that any woman could treat his approach to love-making with such disdain.

Anne didn't care what he thought any more. Didn't care if he did nothing or said nothing. The need for total destruction rolled relentlessly through her mind.

She freed her hair from its constriction, raked her fingers through the thick coil, then shook her head, making the long tresses spill around her shoulders.

"Is that better? More to your liking, Thady? You prefer the sensual, accessible look in your women?"

His mouth thinned into a grimace of painful distaste but he didn't look away. His eyes were glued to her.

Anne unbuttoned her blouse, drew it off her arms, dropped it on the floor. She felt a primitive thrill of triumph when Thady's gaze fell to the soft swell of her breasts above the lacy line of her petticoat. The glass he held tipped, spilling champagne onto his fingers. He seemed not to notice.

"Stop it," he said thickly.

"You started it, Thady. I'm simply delivering what you asked for. What you wanted."

"For God's sake, Anne! Not like this."

"You prefer to pretend, do you, Thady? Do you think that is in better taste?" She unzipped her skirt and slid it down over her hips. "Why don't you come over here and start undressing? Or would that be too *equal* for you?"

She stepped out of her skirt with cool disdain while the rage inside her burnt more fiercely. The scourge of seven years' desertion, then his wanting sex with her on the first day back, drove her onwards.

"Anne." It was a strained plea.

"Am I spoiling it for you?" she railed bitterly at him. "Would you rather have something less direct? Do tell me if it's sensuality that turns you on, Thady. The feel of silk and lace..."

She ran her hands up the slippery fabric of her petticoat and cupped her breasts. "Should I leave my underwear on for you?"

"I told you to stop it, Anne!" Hoarse vehemence.

She kicked off her shoes and turned towards the bed, meaning to set her foot on it while she rolled down her stocking. The shattering of glass halted her in mid-action.

"I said stop it!"

At the harsh command, she jerked her head towards the man who had given it. He was no longer holding a glass of champagne. His hands were fiercely clenched at his sides. His chest was heaving. His eyes blazed with warring passions.

A cold, deadly calm settled over Anne's inner rage. "Something wrong, Thady?"

He exploded into movement as though her taunt had released a compressed spring inside him. "*What* made you like this? *Who* did this to you?" The questions burst from his lips as he covered the short distance between them. He grabbed her arms, fingers biting deep as he shook her. "Was it Tom Colby?"

The mad irony of the questions snapped something inside Anne's head. Her brittle control fell apart. Her voice shook with outrage. "Don't you dare blame Tom for this. I was a person to him. Not just a…" She choked on a welling lump of other emotions. Tears spurted into her eyes.

"If it wasn't Tom Colby, then who was it?"

It was you, you who did this to me, her mind screamed at him. But somehow she couldn't bring herself to say the damning words.

"Anne, tell me who it was who hurt you so badly."

She began to tremble with reaction. What had she done? "It's better if you don't know," she choked out.

"Why?"

Tears overflowed, spilling down her cheeks. The constriction in her throat made speech impossible. She shook her head.

"Anne..."

With a tortured groan he wrapped his arms around her and crushed her to the solid warmth of his body, rocking her as though she were a child who needed the security of being held. He rubbed her back, stroked her hair, every touch imparting an agonised caring that plunged Anne into utter confusion. Was it for *her?* Or was it simply compassion for another person in distress?

All she really knew was how good it felt with him holding her like this. It was so easy to rest her head on his shoulder, to close her eyes and simply give herself to his keeping. She wasn't sure if the trembling weakness inside her was a reaction to what had gone before or a response to what was happening now. Somehow it didn't seem to matter.

It didn't bother her when Thady started trailing soft kisses over her hair. They were warm, gentle, conjuring up memories of how it had been with Thady in the past. She sighed in contentment. She felt his chest expand, felt a shudder run through him. Then his hand slid down to the pit of her back, lower, and she felt the beginning of his arousal.

Before she could even think what she should do about it, he wrenched himself away from her, stepping back, holding her at arm's length. "Get dressed!'' he commanded gruffly, his face tight with strain, his eyes sick with wanting.

''Thady...'' It was a plea for understanding, but sheer confusion prevented any clarity of thought.

''For God's sake! I'm only human, Anne! Cover yourself up before I—'' He made a sound of aversion and spun away, striding forcefully towards the dining setting on the far side of the room.

She watched him go to the bar. He yanked the top off a bottle of whisky, splashed some into a glass. The hand that lifted the glass to his lips was trembling. He took a few quick gulps, shook his head, drank the rest in one fell swoop.

''The door over there leads to a bathroom. Help yourself to whatever you need,'' he said in a deadly monotone, not turning around to look at her.

There was a rigid finality in the stiffness of his back. Thady would not have her now, no matter what she said or did. She had achieved what she set out to achieve. She had given him memories that hurt. And it was indeed ended ... with cold ashes.

She felt like the living dead as she went about getting dressed. She took her handbag and hairpins into the bathroom for the final tidy up. When she emerged, her professional appearance intact again, there was no glow of anticipation in her amber eyes. She knew, with a burrowing sense of loss, that there was nothing to anticipate.

Thady was standing where she had stood before, staring out at the harbour view. She doubted that he was seeing any more than she had. He had an intensely alone air that suggested a complete and utter detachment from the world around him.

"I'm sorry." The words spilled from Anne's lips without any conscious thought of why she should apologise to him.

He turned. There was a haunted look in his eyes that twisted her heart. His mouth moved stiffly into a wry little smile.

"Nothing for you to be sorry about. You simply proved what I've known all along. I'm the wrong man for you."

"Then why did you pursue it?"

He shrugged. "A man can fool himself. When he wants to enough."

She shook her head. "I don't understand you, Thady."

"I don't pretend to understand myself."

It was a glib reply. When her eyes flatly challenged it, a violent distaste twisted across his face.

"Let it go, Anne," he commanded harshly, then made a visible effort to recover a calm composure. He waved towards the dining table, where everything was set for their lunch. "Will you have something to eat now?"

"No, thank you." To stay and eat anything in these circumstances was utterly impossible. Anne knew the invitation was only a bridging politeness. "There's nothing more to be said or done, Thady. I'll go now."

He didn't argue. It was finished, and it was too much a strain on both of them to keep raking over dead ashes.

"I'll see you to a taxi," he offered.

"No. I'd rather you didn't." She fought the stupid tears that were pricking her eyes. "I'll let myself out. Goodbye, Thady."

"La comedia e finita," he quoted softly.

They were the bitter words spoken by the tragic clown at the end of the opera *I Pagliacci,* when his beloved wife lay dead by his own hand.

Destroying what he had most loved.

Did Thady understand what she had set out to do? Or was he referring to what he'd done himself?

Anne stared at him for one further moment, but whichever way the line was read, it was the truth. The play was finished. It was time to ring the curtain down, the cue for her exit from Thady Riordan's life.

She left without another word, closing the door on all that might have been. Yet Anne knew, with a sense of deadly inevitability, that she would be picking over the debris of this day for the rest of her life.

CHAPTER FIVE

ANNE FELT TOTALLY NUMB on the way home. She saw nothing, heard nothing, felt nothing. Like a robot, she automatically registered the necessary movements to get from one place to another. It wasn't until she was inside her small terrace house at Paddington that the numbness started to wear off.

The act of removing her clothes set off the first intense reaction—shivering, as though the temperature had suddenly dropped by twenty degrees. Despite her warmest tracksuit and a heavy woollen jumper, she could do nothing to stop the tremors.

She went downstairs to her workroom in the basement. It was air-conditioned to the same moderate temperature all year round, a necessity for comfortable working conditions because the large belowground room was freezing in winter and like an oven in summer.

She sat down at her desk and listlessly leafed through the sketches for Jenny's wedding party. She was incapable of concentrating on any detail. Her gaze kept drifting to the miniature sets for Thady's play, and her mind fought vainly against bursts of emotional turmoil.

Any kind of involvement with Thady Riordan could not have led anywhere good, she told herself over and over again. That was evident from all that had happened. It was an absurd waste of time thinking about it. Yet Anne could not help feeling that these self-assurances were very hollow.

We share the same passions. The words kept tormenting her no matter how hard she tried to dismiss them. Thady's manner had led her into thinking that he only had sex on his mind, but maybe he had meant a whole range of sharing. The way they thought. The way they worked. A mutual understanding that took away the loneliness they both felt, that went far beyond a togetherness in bed.

Although bed was certainly part of it.

And marriage certainly wasn't.

Thady had flatly stated that he didn't belong in her dreams. He had undoubtedly thought she had given up on them because of her affair with Tom. Such an interpretation was way off the mark.

The truth of the matter was, she had never meant to have an *affair* with Tom Colby. She had simply drifted into it, anticipating the dream of marriage and children and being happy ever after. The illusion that such dreams were possible with Tom was quickly and painfully shattered.

If Thady had been proposing a more serious affair than the strictly sexual encounters he had apparently conducted with those other women, it still fell far short of what Anne wanted. And it was insulting that he should think she would accept it, particularly on the first day of meeting again. It demonstrated the kind of attitude she despised—that a "used" woman was available for sex.

She had definitely done the right thing to cut it dead, although she shuddered with horror every time she remembered how she had gone about it. But it was Thady who had degraded her before she had degraded herself in that mad strip-show. All the same, she was intensely relieved he hadn't followed through on it. She would be hating herself even more now.

Yet maybe that would have been better than brooding over the caring he had shown, the things he had said that indicated she was special to him, at least more special than any other woman over the last seven years. Or had he lied to soften her up, to ease himself over the hump of seven years' desertion?

The room gradually grew darker, the telephone jarring Anne out of her agonising introspection. She stared at the receiver as though it were a coiled snake, ready to strike with deadly venom should she move to touch it. Then a burst of irritation at her paralysed state drove her to snatch it up. Life went on, she fiercely berated herself. It had gone on after Thady Riordan had left her seven years ago, and it would go on now.

"Anne, it's Jenny. How did it go with Thady Riordan?"

The mention of his name was like a stab to the heart, but Anne schooled herself to strain all emotion from her voice. "We met. We talked. It was an experience to remember. That's all." The irony of that truth would be completely lost on her youngest sister.

"Oh!" The sound of disappointment. "Nothing's going to come of it? Not even for your career?"

"Not that I know of."

A big sigh from Jenny. "What a waste! I was hoping to hear some good news."

"Sorry. Clouds with silver linings don't happen very often."

"Maybe you don't look for them," Jenny muttered. "Anyhow, I called to tell you that Brian will drop me at your place on his way to football tomorrow. That'll be after lunch. Okay?"

"Okay. See you then."

The mention of lunch reminded Anne that she hadn't eaten anything since morning. The thought of food had no appeal but she went up to the kitchen and made herself an omelette. It slid down her throat easily enough, although it didn't sit well on her stomach. Sick with nervous exhaustion, she decided. Feeling a desperate need to be finished with this day, she took a sleeping tablet and went to bed.

If anything, Anne felt even more wretched the next day. The night had been a torment of memories. Thady's eyes haunted her dreams of need, loneliness and deep, dark passions.

It was a relief to wake to the morning light of Saturday even though she felt like a limp wrung-out rag. It was also some comfort to know that she would have her sister's company for some of the day. Besides, the inevitable talk about Jenny's wedding would be a continual and salutory reminder to Anne that Thady Riordan's needs and loneliness and desires fell short of wanting a wife.

At one o'clock, Brian Clark, Jenny's devoted fiancé, delivered Anne's youngest sister to her door. Brian was a pleasant young man, a master bricklayer by trade, with the tanned skin and physique that went with his outdoors way of life. He had all the confidence of a twenty-four-year-old who knew where he was going and what he wanted.

He and Jenny swapped a few teasing remarks before he kissed her goodbye and left to go to the football match with his friends. Observing the young couple together, Anne couldn't help wondering if there was a time for such confidence in making a future together, a time that was already past for her. Even though she was only twenty-eight, they made her feel old.

It was obvious that Brian thought the world of Jenny, and there was certainly no doubt that Jenny thought Brian was the answer to all her dreams. Once he had gone, she chattered non-stop about him while Anne made coffee in the kitchen.

Anne could not repress a little stab of envy. To be so happy, to be so in love, to be so sure her love was returned, how good it must feel! Jenny's pretty face was alight with it, her brown eyes sparkling, her skin glowing, her mouth wreathed in continual smiles. Even when she complained that her bouncy blonde hair wasn't growing fast enough for the style she wanted for her wedding, she was unable to look displeased about it.

Once they were settled at Anne's desk in the basement workroom, Jenny's bubbly happiness was entirely focused on the sketches for the wedding dress. She was thrilled with everything Anne set in front of her, her delight increasing with the discussion of detail, choice of fabric, type of veil, accessories.

By mid-afternoon they were going over the designs once more, working out cost estimates. Anne had the contacts to get the fabrics at wholesale prices and she was calculating the total cost for the wedding dress when the door chimes rang.

"Would you get that please, Jenny?" she asked distractedly.

Jenny was up and gone in a flash while Anne concentrated on working out precise figures. It vaguely occurred to her that it was probably Brian returned from his football match. She took no notice of the interruption until she heard Jenny's voice say, "Come this way, please."

She looked up.

Jenny was leading a visitor down the stairs to the basement. The person behind her wore shoes and trousers that could only belong to a man. Each step revealed more about him. He wore a grey suit. A huge bunch of spring flowers rested on the crook of one arm. Curly black hair tumbled over his collar.

Anne's heart clenched as he reached the foot of the staircase. He was the last person in the world she expected to see. When he turned, his gaze swept directly to where she sat at her desk. His eyes caught hers, compelling in their darkly intimate search for a response that would not turn him away.

Anne sat like a stone, incapable of doing anything but staring at him.

Thady Riordan had once more walked into her life.

CHAPTER SIX

"IT'S MR. RIORDAN, ANNE. Mr. *Thady* Riordan," Jenny announced, excitement bubbling through her voice. She was innocently enjoying the impact of his unexpected visit on Anne, and was clearly anticipating a show of pleasure.

It did not come.

In reply to her sister, Anne simply said, "Thank you, Jenny."

The flat words belied the whirling storm in her mind, the irrepressible ache of hope in her heart, the despair of knowing there was no possible future to be forged from this meeting.

Yesterday had seen to that. Tom Colby had seen to that. And so had Thady Riordan. So why had he come? What could he possibly hope to gain from seeing her again?

He walked towards her, the arc of tension between them tightening with each step. Anne was vaguely aware that Jenny held back, apparently sensitive to an atmosphere that totally excluded her. Thady didn't attempt a smile. Nor did he bother with any facile words for social ease. His face was set in tight determination, his shoulders straight, his whole bearing one of resolute purpose, and his eyes burned with the resolution to carry that purpose forward no matter what the odds and what the cost.

Anne remained totally still, waiting, watching, silently agonising over all that had happened between them. A treacherous little hope kept whispering that this was another chance, that maybe this time...

"I hope you don't mind my coming here, Anne," Thady said softly. "I wanted to say a final goodbye to you. I'll be flying back to London in the morning."

Any last possible hope crumbled. "Hasn't everything been said, Thady?"

"No." He shook his head as he advanced the last few steps to the other side of her desk. "I couldn't leave without apologising. Without saying how sorry I am that I've hurt you. Without doing something to restore what I've taken from you. Without asking for your forgiveness."

"You didn't take anything from me. You don't need my forgiveness," she retorted fiercely, denying her need for the love he would never give her and hating the memory of what he had offered her and she had offered him.

He laid the massed array of flowers on the desk in front of her with the slow deliberation of a petitioner laying an offering on a church altar. His fingers trailed gently over the vibrantly coloured petals of daffodils and poppies. His gaze lifted from them to look at her with pained regret.

"Words do not always express what the heart feels. I wanted to give you these flowers to remind you that even after the most bitter winter, spring does come. I didn't mean to hurt you as I did, Anne. I was anxious, overeager, too wrapped up in my own needs. I'm deeply sorry for the blind selfishness that drove me to pursue something that was always going to be destructive to you."

He paused, seemed to take stock of himself and the situation. His mouth curved, but not into a smile. Rather reminiscent of the light and sweetness they had both known so many years ago. "I always thought of you as spring. That was the time of year we spent together. I guess I want to think that spring can come again for you, with all its warm promise of something new and beautiful."

Anne was both moved and deeply hurt by this farewell gesture. It was the hurt that rose uppermost and spilled from her tongue. "Lovely words, Thady, but that's all they are. Words!" The need to challenge all he had done to her broke into voice, harsh and insistent. "Tell me why spring can't come for you?"

A bleak weariness, colourless and infinite, dragged over his face. "There are some things that no power on earth can change, Anne." His mouth twisted sardonically. "What I can do is strictly limited to what is within my power to do."

"Like leaving me to my fate," Anne mocked. She felt a burst of bitter anger against this further emotion-tearing intrusion into her life. "Why pretend you care about what I feel, Thady? Why did you bother coming back to Australia? Why the hell did you bother coming here today?"

Suddenly she was on her feet and sweeping the flowers from her desk with a swing of her arm that sent Jenny's sketches fluttering after them. "I don't want your guilty conscience!"

"Anne!" Jenny's shocked gasp and move forward was a jolting reminder of her presence.

"Stay out of this, Jenny," Anne commanded through clenched teeth. Some self-protective instinct urged she keep Jenny nearby, yet Anne could not bear any overt interference in this last confrontation.

"That's all this is, isn't it?" she raged on at Thady, her amber eyes blazing in savage accusation. "I made you feel bad yesterday, and you didn't like it. So before you flew off out of *my* life, back to *your* life in London, you wanted to make yourself feel better and you wanted me to feel worse."

His head jerked in an anguished negative, but he made no other move. His face had gone deadly pale but seemed to have tightened in its resolution. "No," he answered quietly. "What I feel doesn't matter and never has."

She couldn't bear the sadness and gentleness in his eyes. It accused her of not understanding him, and all her tortured emotions twisted into a desperate need to know the truth. "Did you ever care about me?"

"Yes."

"Tell me one thing you ever did that showed you really cared about me!"

"Anne . . ." Something dreadful warred across his face. He lifted a hand in appeal, dropped it, then half-turned away.

"You can't tell me one thing, can you? It's all been a pose to get what you want. Whatever that is. I don't understand you. I never have. I never will. I want to forget you, forget you ever existed." She gave a harsh laugh. "What a marvellous sense of freedom you must feel, Thady, that you can afford to fly around the world for a one-night stand!"

He spun to face her, his eyes searing hers with naked need. "I wanted to be with you. I wanted you to be with me." His voice shook with passion. Then his hands sliced a violent dismissal. "What I did was wrong. I know I was wrong. But don't say I haven't cared, Anne. I've always cared."

He saw her blank disbelief.

It goaded him into a further passionate declaration. "I gave you the career you wanted. It was the one dream that I could do something about."

She shook her head in fierce denial. "I got to where I am on my own. You had nothing to do with it, Thady. Nothing!"

"Contacts are everything in this business, Anne. You know that. Without—"

"Alex Korbett saw my production design for *Godspell*. He offered me a job because I had the kind of talent and skills he was looking for. He saw that for himself. It had nothing to do with you."

"What was Alex Korbett doing at a show put on by an amateur musical theatre group, Anne? Why do you imagine he was there to see your work, to see your talent, to see your skill?"

Anne froze. She remembered how she had thought it an amazing and incredible stroke of luck at the time. She had involved herself with amateur theatre ever since her school days, always on the production side of things. She had been very proud of her work on *Godspell*, and she had asked Thady to the opening night. He had been enthusiastic about it. It had been a wonderful night together.

It had also been their last night together. Although she hadn't known it then. She remembered how she had bubbled over with excitement because of the marvellous response from the audience. She remembered Thady looking at her in a different way, and she had thought it meant a breakthrough in their friendship, that he was seeing her more as an equal, that he wouldn't hold back from her any more.

She had been so hopelessly wrong. He did more than hold back. He left Australia without saying goodbye, without seeing her again.

"You told Alex Korbett about me before you went away?" she choked out.

"I pressed Alex to take you on as his assistant. I used all the influence I could bring to bear on him. I bribed him with a case of his favourite champagne to go and see your *Godspell*. I offered to pay your wages for a trial period of a year."

"You paid him?" she cried in pained protest.

"Alex wasn't looking for an assistant, Anne. He didn't need one."

It was all fixed, Anne thought dully. What she had achieved was worthless. The miracle that had started her in her career had been no miracle at all. Alex Korbett attending the last night of the show, coming backstage to find her, introducing himself, giving her his card, offering her a job as his assistant...everything arranged and paid for by Thady Riordan.

"So what you're telling me...all I've achieved is owing to your intervention on my behalf," she forced out, feeling so sick she could barely keep standing.

"No. You did it on your own merits, Anne. I merely gave you the opportunity."

"How can I ever be sure of that now?"

"Because you've proved your talent over and over again. You were better than anyone could ever have anticipated. That was why Alex made a point of coming to see me when he was in London. It was simply to tell me all about you, what had happened to you, the exciting prospects he had held out for you. He also gave me back the money I'd paid him. And two cases of champagne."

She felt numb all over. What had possessed Thady to do what he had done? "I suppose...I should thank you."

"It was the least I could do for you in the circumstances."

Her eyes raked his in her naked need for the truth. "A consolation prize for losing the lover I wanted?"

"Anne..." He looked sick. "It wouldn't have worked out. Not then." He grimaced. "Not ever."

"Then what was yesterday about, Thady? Getting something back for all I owed you?"

He shook his head tiredly. "If you want to believe that of me, then do so. But you need have no fear that you'll ever be asked for such *payment* again."

"The *final* goodbye," she muttered, more to herself than him.

"Yes," he affirmed, his voice a low, gravelly rasp. "I need to get on with writing again." He dragged in a deep breath and continued in a more controlled tone. "You asked why I bothered coming back to Australia. It was to see your production design for my play."

He drew an envelope from the inner breast pocket of his suit coat and laid it on the desk in front of Anne. "This is a fax of a contract drawn up by my solicitors in London. It came through early this morning. If you sign it as an interim measure until the original arrives, it will give you the right to the stage design of all future productions of my plays, no matter where they are performed in the world."

Anne felt the blood draining from her face as she stared at the envelope that promised to make her name in production design all around the world. Thady was not merely opening a door of opportunity, he was ensuring her career in a way that guaranteed success at a level she had never dreamed of.

Her mind ran over all the implications. Her heart screamed its protest at how inexorably she would be tied to Thady Riordan if she signed. He would always be part of her life, even though they might never meet again.

"I can't accept—"

"It's for my benefit, Anne, not yours," he argued softly. "Having seen what you can do, I don't want anyone else working on my plays."

"No. It's worth a small fortune. It's too much—"

"It's worth a small fortune to me to have my plays presented as you alone can present them. There's no favour involved in this. It's strictly a professional decision, Anne. I want the best. You are the best."

She dragged her gaze up to his and met only a steadfast resolve.

"You won't be dealing with me in any shape or form," he assured her. "My agent will handle all business details. As it happens, my next play is ready to go into production, so you'll need to be in London by the end of next week. I've written down everything you need to know once you get there. The contacts I've already set up for you—"

"Thady, you can't—"

"Yes, I can. It's done, Anne. There's an airline ticket for you in the envelope. Also the keys to a flat in Knightsbridge. The lease has over two years to run so there's no worry for you about where to stay."

"It's too much," she protested in painful confusion.

"You told me that the most important thing in your life is your career," he reminded her with relentless purpose. Then his voice softened. "Don't let what I did yesterday influence you against taking this up, Anne. There are no strings attached to it. The contract is watertight. Sign it. And show the theatre-going world what Annelise Tolliver can do."

Her eyes filled with tears as she looked at him with all the unfulfilled yearning in her soul. Pride didn't matter any more. He was making himself unreachable, and this was the last she would ever see of him. The green eyes with their dark hidden passions. The strong face that would always be stamped in her memory. The softness of the tumbling black curls. The tenderness she had known from him.

His lashes swept down, veiling whatever he was feeling as he reached into his pocket again and brought out a little box wrapped in gold paper. He laid it on top of the envelope.

"A small gift," he said huskily. "I hope, sometime in the future . . . years from now . . . you might look at something I gave you and remember me kindly."

His eyes seared hers before he turned and strode away from her. He was leaving. Leaving forever. And Anne's whole body reacted in violent protest. She had to speak, had to stop him.

"Thady, wait."

He paused. His back stiffened. He resumed walking away from her.

"Don't go," she pleaded.

He reached the foot of the staircase.

"Is it your need to write that makes you do these things to me?" she cried, grasping at any straw in her need to understand him.

He paused again, longer this time, his hands clenching and unclenching as he seemed to grope for an answer. "Yes," he said simply, barely audible.

"Are you then totally selfish, Thady Riordan?" she hurled at him, fighting his retreat from her every inch of the way.

His back was still turned to her. She saw his shoulders heave as he sucked in a deep breath. His hand curled around the newel post, knuckles gleaming white. "Yes. Totally selfish," he said harshly. "I have my destiny to fulfil, just as you have yours. It's best that you think of it that way."

"Don't tell me what's best for me!" Anne retorted fiercely. "You don't know what's best for me!"

He started up the stairs, ignoring her claim, not looking at her.

"Don't go," she begged. "Not yet."

His head turned. His eyes raked her face and body with a raw desire that made her flesh prickle with heat. "I could not repress my *sexual* feelings," he said bitterly. "You remind me all too earnestly that I'm the kind of man you don't want any part of."

"What if I do want what you want?" she answered recklessly.

"You don't, Anne. And I could not bear a repetition of yesterday."

She had no answer to that. The memory throbbed between them in all its bitter horror.

"I *must* go, Anne," Thady said quietly. "There is no more I can do for you."

There was not so much as a further fleeting glance from him as he moved swiftly up the stairs. She caught only a glimpse of grimly set features. Then he was gone. Having done all he could for her. Having made his final goodbye.

A convulsive shiver ran through Anne, followed by an unnerving attack of trembling. She sank onto her chair. She stared at the envelope and the little gold box on top of it. She reached out and touched them, wanting, needing to feel something of Thady in them. But they were cold and lifeless.

Tears welled in her eyes, and she did not have the strength to force them back or blink them away. She buried her face in her hands and wept, her heart pouring out its grief for all that had been taken beyond her reach.

CHAPTER SEVEN

A GENTLE TOUCH on her hair jerked Anne out of her heart-broken misery. She looked up to find Jenny standing beside her. Jenny, whose presence she had completely forgotten. The realisation that her younger sister had witnessed everything was another agonising truth to absorb. With an anguished moan she dropped her head back into her hands.

"Leave me, please," she sobbed. "I want to be alone."

Her sister's hand went on softly stroking, trying to impart loving comfort. "Anne, I can't leave you like this. Please . . . I want to help."

"Nothing can help." It was a cry of bottomless despair.

"Don't say that, Anne. I can't bear it. And I'm sure it can be made right."

Jenny's arm came around her shoulders, giving her a tight hug. They had never been a demonstrative family. They all knew what they felt but they rarely showed it. Somehow Jenny's demonstration of love and concern made Anne feel worse. She had always been the one to give love and consolation to her younger sisters. To have Jenny, the youngest of all, doing this for her only pointed out more clearly the hopelessness of her case.

"It can't be made right, Jenny," she choked out.

"Why not?"

"Because Thady wants what Tom Colby had with me. And I gave Tom Colby nothing but pain. I couldn't love him the way he wanted to be loved."

"But that was because you still loved Thady Riordan, Anne. Love is the most tearing, blinding, passionate emotion...."

"Thady doesn't want my love. He wants...only what he wants."

"No. He does want your love, Anne. It half-killed him to walk away from you."

"You don't understand."

"I do. Brian and I have had our fights, our disagreements. Everyone does."

"Not like this."

"Anne, you have to accept that the person you love isn't perfect. No-one is. You have to accept Thady as he is. I think you've tried to shut him out because he didn't fulfil your expectations when you wanted him to. You've made a habit of shutting us all out."

"I don't shut you out." She raised pained, tear-laden eyes. "If you ever needed me for anything..."

"You gave it to us," Jenny finished for her. "All of us. And we love you for it. But, Anne, that's not the same as letting us into *your* life. You let us think all that mattered to you was your career. But that's not true, is it?"

"Oh, Jenny! That's all there is for me. That's all I've got left."

"Anne, it's so obvious now," Jenny said softly, sadly. "*He's* the only man you ever loved. *He's* why you've never married. All these years of lonely heartache... You never gave a hint of it. You never let us help you."

Anne shook her head wearily. "There was no point."

"I suddenly feel we haven't known you. That you're a stranger."

"Nothing's changed." Anne released a deep sigh, mopped up her tears and lifted her head, looking at Jenny with bleak resignation. "Nothing is going to change. I'm a career woman. That *is* it, Jenny. That's all I've got."

Jenny looked at her with sympathy and deeply anxious concern. "Because of Thady."

Anne gave a harsh, mirthless laugh. "Without Thady, I'd never have got started." Dully she reached out and picked up the envelope he had left behind. "And now he's lifting me to the heights. All I have to do is sign his contract."

"I think Thady Riordan loves you, Anne."

The painful constriction in her chest seemed to tighten. "I don't know what he feels for me, Jenny. It's not what Brian feels for you."

"People are passionate because they care, Anne. Thady is passionate about you, and Brian is passionate about me. They both care for us very deeply."

"Thady cares about his writing. That's what he cares about most."

Jenny moved to take Anne's hand and press it hard, compelling her attention. Deep conviction was in her voice. "You're wrong, Anne. You didn't see his face when you asked if it was his writing that made him do what he has to you. I saw his face. I saw what was written on it. It was pure agony. He was lying to you, Anne."

"Why should he lie?" Anne shook her head in mocking dismissal of Jenny's contention. "He left me the same as he did before. Except this time he said goodbye. And he said he would never see me again."

"He didn't want to leave," Jenny retorted. "He made himself do it. He was lying about being totally selfish, too. I'm as sure of that as I have been of anything in my life. If he hadn't had his back turned to you, if you'd seen his face, Anne, you'd know that what I'm saying is true."

"Why? Why would he do such a thing?"

"I don't know. Perhaps..." Jenny frowned and shook her head. "That may be too fanciful."

"Tell me!"

"Have you ever thought he may be protecting you?"

"From what? What do I need protection from?"

"I'm not sure," Jenny said slowly. "Maybe..."

"Yes?"

Jenny searched her eyes anxiously. "Could it be that he's protecting you from something within himself?

Something he knows he can't change, not even for you?"

The wrong man... some things no power on earth can change...

"But he could have tried to explain," Anne reasoned.

Why couldn't he have appealed to her understanding instead of making judgments? How was she supposed to overlook such a basic failure in communication? He didn't care enough about her. He couldn't. And yet why had he done all he'd done for her?

"He's not selfish, Anne," Jenny said, as though picking up on Anne's thoughts. "How can he be selfish when he cared enough to start you in your career? And this contract. You may be the best, but I bet he would have given it to you anyway."

Anne dragged in a deep breath, trying to relieve the awful tightness in her chest. She looked down the room to the miniature stage sets on the workbench. Thady's destiny. And hers. Tied together, but somehow always apart.

"Whatever Thady feels for me, Jenny, believe you me, it's not the kind of love that leads to marriage."

"I don't know. I can't answer that."

Anne heard the caring anguish in Jenny's voice, but there was no escaping the truth. "He wants sex with me."

"For God's sake, Anne! Is there something wrong with that? Isn't it natural when two people feel deeply about each other?"

I wanted to be with you. I wanted you to be with me....

Thady's words haunted her. But for how long would he want that? He had said straight out that whatever they had together would ultimately be destructive to her. He believed that. He truly believed it was best for her that he stay right out of her life. Although he wasn't out of her life, and never would be, except in the physical sense. If she signed the contract it would bond them all the closer, even though she would never see him again.

"What happened yesterday?" Jenny asked quietly. "Or is that too intrusive a question?"

Anne turned to her, bitter ashes in her mouth. "He gave me a proposition. I threw it back in his face. A proposition, Jenny, not a proposal. And he made it clear that that was all he would ever offer me."

Jenny winced in sympathy, reached out and tenderly stroked Anne's hair from her face. "He might change his mind if you give him another chance."

Anne shook her head. "It's not so simple, Jenny. You don't know how it was. And I could never explain it."

"I don't know what went on between you and Thady yesterday, but I know what I saw today, Anne. That man cares for you. *Really* cares for you."

Jenny stepped back and began slowly picking up the flowers and papers that were strewn across the floor. "You can say it's none of my business," she continued quietly, "but I want to see you happy, Anne. Like you used to be when you were my age. I don't want to see you eating your heart out. Anything would be better than that.''

"Jenny, I tried to stop him from leaving," Anne muttered defeatedly. "He's made up his mind. There's no turning the clock back."

"You can turn it forward."

"You don't know Thady. He retreats inside himself where no-one can reach him."

"Whatever barriers he's been putting up between you, I can tell you this—they were cracking all over the place this afternoon. He's like a dam, and that dam was about ready to burst."

Jenny straightened up, laid the papers and the flowers on the desk and eyed Anne with a very adult look of measured calculation. "What have you got to lose? You don't want any other man. If he's the only one for you, why not go to him and give him another chance? He's not leaving for London until tomorrow."

Tears blurred Anne's eyes again.

"Oh, Anne..." Jenny flung her arms around her and rubbed her cheek affectionately over Anne's bent head. "I want everything to be right for you. The way it is for me and Brian. It's not impossible, is it?"

Thady had already done what he believed was right for her. It was too late to turn that decision into something else. They had both acknowledged that yesterday. Thady had confirmed it beyond any doubt today. The final goodbye was *final*. If she went to him now, she'd be asking him to do something he felt was wrong.

The door chimes rang.

"That will be Brian," Jenny said.

Anne caught her hand as Jenny began to withdraw her arms. She pressed it with compelling urgency. "Please don't invite him in, Jenny. Leave with him. I'm not up to... to socialising."

"I could tell him to come back later."

"No. I don't want..." She twisted around to appeal to her sister. "Jenny, please don't talk about this to the family. I can bear it alone. I can't... I'd hate for them to know. I'd rather them think I have my—" she forced a wobbly smile "—my brilliant career."

"If that's what you want, Anne."

"Thank you, Jenny. I'll ring you on Monday night about the dresses."

"It's not urgent. It's not important if..." Her face reflected anxious concern. "Will you consider what I said about Thady, Anne? I truly think he loves you. If you opened up and told him..."

"I'll think about it," Anne said dully, not wanting to invite further argument.

Jenny leaned down and kissed her cheek. "Remember we love you," she murmured. "You've always been special to me, Anne. Whatever you decide, that will be the right decision, and I'll always love you."

Anne couɪd make no reply. She blundered to her feet, blindly reaching out to embrace her little sister and hug her close.

The door chimes rang again.

She stroked Jenny's silky blonde hair, the baby of the family, the sweet natural one who had always taken it on trust that everybody loved her. "Go," Anne whispered. "Go and be happy with the man you love."

Jenny drew back. They exchanged wobbly smiles. Anne watched her sister run up the stairs. Then she sank onto her chair.

In front of her on the desk were Thady's gifts—the little gold box, the envelope containing her future career, the keys to a flat in London and the massed array of spring flowers. She reached out and gently trailed her fingers over the soft fragrant petals. *The warm promise of something new and beautiful.*

But there were no promises from Thady.

Only offerings.

A gift so that she might remember him kindly.

A contract to further her career.

And whatever was meant by *sharing the same passions.*

Slowly Anne gathered up the flowers and carried them upstairs to the kitchen. She filled a plastic bucket with water, then set the flowers in it. Into every life some rain must fall, she thought. Rain to let the flowers grow.

She hoped the sun would shine on Jenny on her wedding day. For herself, it didn't matter so much anymore.

The thought came to her that she would rather have rain with Thady than all the sunshine in the world on her own. And who knew what flowers might grow in that rain? Brief. Ephemeral. But like so many of the transient things in life, those flowers could be the most beautiful of all. She could try keeping them alive. Why not? Any kind of life with him had to be better than the emotional winter she faced without him.

With her mind working feverishly over how best to change Thady's mind, Anne headed for the bathroom. She needed to take a shower. She needed to wash her hair, her beautiful hair....

CHAPTER EIGHT

ANNE KNOCKED on the door to Thady's suite at the Park Hyatt. Her knuckles echoed the resounding thud of her heart. In her other hand she held the envelope and the little gold box, ready for Thady to see that they remained unopened. She had her speech rehearsed. She was ready. But when her knock was not answered, the words were dispersed by fear.

She stared at the door, which remained shut to her. Was she locked out of Thady's life forever? Was she too late? Had he already left the hotel?

She knocked again. Harder. Longer. Louder.

The door opened.

He wore one of the thick white bathrobes the hotel supplied to guests. His face was half turned aside. Apparently he was expecting to admit a maid. His demeanour was one of complete disinterest with the world in general. Anne saw his body instantly stiffen at the sight of her. A tense wariness wiped the weariness from his face.

"May I come in?" She spoke the words out of conventional politeness. The door was open. Before he could think of saying anything or denying her entry, Anne brushed straight past him, putting him between her and the door, swiftly and decisively gaining the space she needed to feel safe inside his domain.

"I needed to see you again, Thady," she rushed on, talking fast to claim his attention. "There are a number of things about the contract I need to get straight with you."

She heard the door closing behind her. Her sense of relief at this initial acceptance was so intense she began to shake.

"What things, Anne?"

The terseness, even cynicism in his voice told her he wanted this over and done with as fast as possible. She took a deep breath, struggling for the control she needed to get through this ordeal with him, to convince him she meant what she said. Her heart had leapt into a chaotic rhythm. She forced her legs to walk a few more steps into the lounge area of the suite before she turned to face him.

He stood in the small passageway to the door, obviously intent on cutting this visit to the minimum necessities. The grim set of his face made him look older than his thirty-four years. The green eyes were narrowed to dark slits.

He did not look at the luxuriant fall of her honey-brown hair flowing softly over her shoulders. She might have been wearing rags for what little notice he took of her rich gold cashmere sweater and brown velvet slacks. He appeared totally unaware of the manner in which they clung sensually to all the feminine curves of her body. She had a sense of him deliberately blocking out her sexuality, reducing his vision to a narrow tunnel that saw only a problem to be solved and eliminated.

Anne fiercely repressed all the doubts and fears that tore at her resolution. This was the last chance, the only opportunity she would ever get. She had to seize it. She saw his gaze drop to the envelope and the little gold box she held out to him, saw him frown over the fact that neither had been opened.

"It's no good, Thady," she started softly. "I don't want to work on your plays without talking to you and seeing you. I need to see you and talk to you. I need to be with you."

"No, you don't, Anne," he replied decisively. "You can manage quite superbly without any input from me. This last production design you did—"

"Was sheer hell for me!" she cut in, silencing him with her vehemence. "It was a constant living reminder of what I didn't have. I don't want to have known you briefly. I don't want to remember you kindly. I *need* to have you in my life. I want to be with you. I want to know you. And taking these things from you—"

She tossed his contract and gift onto the nearest armchair. "I can't do it. They'd only make the wanting worse. Because they'd keep reminding me of all I don't have. I *need* you, Thady."

For a moment there was stunned disbelief on his face.

"Ever since you left me seven years ago, my life has been empty," Anne continued, her voice trembling with the force of her emotion. "I filled it with the career you gave me. I don't know if you've ever met Tom Colby. He's like you in many superficial ways. I fooled myself into thinking I was in love with him. Simply because you weren't there, Thady."

"No." It was little more than a breath of denial coming from lips that had gone bone dry.

Tears sprang into her eyes. Words kept spilling from her lips. "I caused Tom pain through no fault of his own. He couldn't fill your shoes. I caused myself pain. Perhaps I even caused you pain. I'm sorry. Sorry for everything I did."

"Anne." He lifted his hand in some tortured appeal. A haunted look came into his eyes. "For God's sake! Say that isn't true."

"You don't have to love me, Thady," she rushed on, hearing the desperation creeping into her voice. She was unable to suppress it. "As long as you care a little about me. And I'm not just a woman you need to use occasionally."

"God, no! No!" He shook his head in anguished protest at the revelations that were pouring from her. "Don't say it was because of me. I tried... I left before it went too far."

"What's too far, Thady?"

"Nothing happened between us."

"Too much had happened. Too much that was unforgettable to me."

"No!" His hand sliced the air as though he was warding off what she was pressing on him. "I can still hurt you, Anne. It's hard enough that I can't be what you want me to be."

"I don't want you to be anything but what you are, Thady. I swear that I'll never try to change what you are," Anne pleaded, afraid of losing this encounter, afraid of losing him. "Please. Can't we share things together like we used to?"

He sent a searing look over her body as his mouth twisted into a savage mockery of what she was suggesting.

"I meant for us to be lovers, as well," she added, urgently correcting what she had just said. "I meant it to be that way seven years ago, and I mean it now."

He slowly lifted his gaze to hers, challenging her desire with the rawness of reality. "You think I could take you after yesterday? That I'm an animal with no conscience at all about hurting you, Anne?"

"I want you to take me," she answered simply. "That's part of being in love. It's only natural. I want to share everything that is possible between us, Thady. As man and woman. As lovers. As friends. As professionals working together for the same purpose. To create things. To achieve. Couldn't we try that, Thady?"

He stared at her as though he were seeing her for the first time. His chest rose and fell quickly as though he needed all the oxygen he could get to clear his mind, to see more clearly.

"And yesterday?" he asked hoarsely.

"I was expressing my hurt, my grief, my anger because you left me and didn't seem to care."

He was deciding whether it was *right* or not, Anne thought with a surge of panic. It drove her to move towards him. She held out her hands to him, appealing, offering, inviting.

"You showed me you did care this afternoon, Thady. If you care for me, please don't shut me out. I *need* you. I'm so lonely...so desperate. I *need* you so much."

Whatever thoughts Thady Riordan had were obliterated by that last despairing cry. His arms opened to accept her, to take her into his embrace. She had said the words that overrode everything else in his life. He could not deny her need.

CHAPTER NINE

RELIEF FLOODED THROUGH Anne as Thady enfolded her in his arms. His body emanated strength. It promised that for however long she was with him like this, there would be no loneliness.

She pressed closer, resting her head against the angle of his neck and shoulder. She listened to the pulsing thud of his heart. His arms tightened around her. His breathing seemed to intensify, becoming deeper, faster. His head brushed against her hair, her beautiful hair, and she felt the warmth of his breath as he trailed his lips over it.

"I'm home," she whispered.

"Yes," he replied huskily.

His tongue traced the outer rim of her ear. He moved one arm down to cement her body against his, then increased the intimacy of their closeness by straddling his legs against her thighs, holding her within the power of his strong masculinity.

"There's no going back from here, Anne."

"I know."

He planted deep, passionate kisses on her neck. She slid a hand up to the open V of his bathrobe, pushed the heavy cloth aside. His flesh was firm and smooth and hot. His shoulder bunched with tense muscle. His hair was a soft tangle of silk. She pressed her lips to the throbbing artery in his throat.

He made a low, guttural sound. A hand swiftly curled around her chin, tilting her head back. His mouth was on hers, his lips moving quickly, persuasively, possessively over hers, pressing for all she would give him.

She surrendered to the craving she felt in every ounce of his body, the rising tension and excitement. As she welcomed the deepening of his kiss, she moved her arms around the top of his shoulders, caressing his neck, revelling in the joy of loving freely, with Thady wanting her, Thady loving her.

She felt the thickness and hardness of his arousal and moved her body sensuously, the seductive call and response of lover to lover. Her head was spinning from lack of air, but that felt right, too, not belonging to herself anymore, whirling into sensation.

Thady's mouth broke away from hers, taking deep, hoarse breaths, his chest heaving. She could feel the rigidity of the muscles in his neck and shoulders, in his stomach and thighs. He picked her up in his arms.

He walked around the suite, carrying her with him, pausing when it suited his purpose. "Turn out the light," he softly commanded at each stop. And while she extended her arm to the switch he indicated with a nod of his head, he kissed her, completely and passionately, sometimes moving straight to the next light switch, sometimes lingering to increase the sensuality of their togetherness.

He came to the last glowing lamp upon the table near the window. "Turn out the light." And while his mouth found hers, her arm extended sightlessly to do what she was bid.

She found the button and pressed it. Darkness cloaked them in a private, intensely intimate world. She thought Thady would take her to the bed, but he didn't. He set her on her feet, not releasing her from the intimacy of the kiss. He straightened up with her, perfectly balanced, helping her to balance with his strength.

Their bodies came together and she felt him tremble, perhaps from exertion or from having his control overcome by unbearable excitement, or both. She clung more tightly to him, running her hands urgently over his body, trying to soothe his tremors. A moan of longing came from his throat. He kissed her with a devouring passion that seemed only to increase the spasms of rippling muscles.

It was the most wonderful thing Anne had ever experienced. She broke away from the pressure of his need, gasping out a plea for his sake. "I want you now, Thady. I want you now."

It seemed to affect him, to steady him. "No." He dragged in a deep breath, shook his head. He stepped aside, reached out for something. Behind her the curtains swished open. "I want you to have everything, Anne," he said softly. "Everything I *can* give you."

He turned her to face the beautiful vista of the harbour, the lights of the city, the shimmering reflections of the water. His arms slid around her waist, gently pulling her against him. He had discarded the bath-robe, and the feel of his warm nakedness burnt through her clothes, exciting a sexual awareness that quivered inward.

"The mystery of the night," he murmured, his mouth grazing erotically over her hair. "So much that is ephemeral, but behind it, the hidden depths of eternity stretching out to the end of time. And we stand here together, live warmth, defying the cold loneliness of all the dark spaces." His hands glided up to caress the soft swell of her breasts. "Earth has nothing more beautiful to offer."

Anne knew intuitively that he didn't mean the night. He meant the sharing, she with him, he with her.

He gathered up the cashmere sweater and the silk camisole she had worn underneath it. She swayed as he lifted the garments over her head and dropped them on the floor. He caught her to him, his hands taking total possession of her breasts as he pressed her bared back to the muscled breadth of his chest, naked skin to skin, hot, vibrant.

Instinctively Anne lifted her hands to cover his, holding them in place over her heart as she leaned her head to one side, then the other, revelling in the passionate rain of Thady's kisses down her neck and across her shoulders, in the sensuous rub of his aroused state against the soft curves of her bottom. Then his hands slid from under hers, dropped to the fastening of her velvet slacks. He snapped it open, undid the zipper. With a smooth action that collected her panties as well, he eased the fabric over her hips, down her thighs, fingers softly stroking the material down.

She stepped out of her shoes, lifted her feet free of the clothes and stood trembling with anticipation as Thady trailed feather-light fingers up her legs, behind her knees, the soft inner flesh of her thighs, the erogenous zones below her hipbones. Her stomach contracted in spasms of excitement as she felt him straighten up behind her.

Again his arms encircled her, pulling her back against him, but the intimacy of his embrace was immeasurably heightened as she felt the hardness of his manhood slide between her thighs, stirring a range of sensations that flooded through her in rippling waves.

There was something intensely primeval in facing the night like that, totally naked, locked in a world of their own, yet looking out at the shifting waves of the harbour, the lights that glowed for other people, the stars of the universe, the darkness beyond. Wrapped within the shelter of Thady's arms, anchored between his legs, rocking to the rhythm of his exquisite stroking.

Anne wanted to see his face, his eyes. It wasn't enough to feel him with her. She needed to know. An image flashed into her mind of Eve reaching for the apple from the Tree of Knowledge, the serpent coiled there ready to strike. It was wrong to question, she told herself. She had to accept. That was what she had said to Thady, that she would accept whatever he was. No turning back from here.

But the brief perturbation of mind had made her heart beat faster. He felt it. As though he knew what she wanted he withdrew from her, turned her around, held her away from him so they could gaze upon each other. In the dim light thrown from beyond the window she could see the brooding intentness with which he looked at her, as though measuring her meaning to him.

"Thady..." His name broke from her lips in a whisper of yearning.

"It's all right," he assured her huskily. "I want the magic of this moment stored in my memory forever. The reality of you as a woman."

He began touching her with mesmerising softness, running his fingertips over her face, down her throat, across her shoulders, tracing the line of her arms to her fingertips, then up again to begin another journey of discovery. Her skin leapt with sensitivity, but the thrill of his touch held her totally captivated. He caressed every inch of her body, moving her to his will.

Only when he bent to kiss the tips of her breasts was the spell he had cast on her broken enough for her to lift her arms and touch him. It seemed right, imperative, to cradle his head there, to make him feel as precious to her as he had made her feel to him. Yet there was a tingling weakness in her arms that robbed her of any power to keep him in her hold. Her fingers slid through the thick curls of his hair as he lowered his head to trail warm kisses over her stomach.

Then he was kneeling in front of her, pleasuring with his touch, his tongue, his lips, searching out and drawing on the very essence of her femininity. Never in her life had Anne imagined anything like this. She arched against the glass of the window as his mouth moved from side to side, his tongue sometimes darting, sometimes caressing, sometimes evoking almost violent sensations. She could bear no more. The need for some final, more complete appeasement racked her entire body. Her fingers raked through his hair, tugging, pulling him up to her in blind, frantic urgency.

He rose, his manhood surging into her with a vibrant pulsation that made her knees collapse. He caught her to him, lifting her, supporting her as he filled her with his own engorged need, and their bodies became one, flesh to flesh in an orgasmic joining that went far, far beyond any simple togetherness.

Somehow Anne found the strength to lock her legs around him as he carried her to the bed. The movement was exquisitely sensational. The rapid heaving of his chest against her breasts created another delicious rhythm of sensitivity. Then the sight of him leaning over her as he knelt on the bed, arranging pillows for her, positioning her to his need, so dominantly powerful in cradling her body against his.

She could feel herself opening further and further to him, welcoming, flowing around him, releasing him only to draw him into more and more sublime intimacy. She felt his muscles spasm, out of control, heard him cry out in agonised pleasure as the ultimate tension of climax gripped him. His whole body convulsed at the final release of all he had held back in giving everything he could to her, but this gift of himself provided the greatest fulfilment.

A sweet flood of warmth permeated Anne's entire body, and even when Thady took her with him to lie on their sides, they stayed locked together, and the flood rolled on and on in rippling waves. It was so beautiful she wanted to keep capturing it, prolonging it. Instinctively she arched away to an angle that allowed her to move in a voluptuous roll around their togetherness.

Her body hummed to an exquisite sexuality that Thady played on, stroking her, fondling her breasts, shaping them to his mouth, drawing on them with a hard sucking that had her writhing with pleasure. Somehow he knew what she wanted, what she needed, intuitively accommodating her every movement, sliding his body against hers, inciting the continuation of intense sensation.

She felt him grow hard again, filling her with the throb of his wanting for more. He pulled her on top of him, his hands feasting on her womanly curves, his mouth claiming her breasts. Anne was filled with a wild need to take him, possess him, submerge herself in nothing but pure woman instinct, pleasuring herself and the man she loved.

If it was madness, it was a madness Thady shared with her and fed to the extremes of experience, leading her to other positions, encouraging and inciting her to feel all there was to feel in the physical intimacies they could take with each other. There were no inhibitions, nothing that was forbidden.

It was as though they were driven to know, to have, to take all they had missed out on in the years apart, as though they only had tonight and there was no tomorrow. The sense of wanting everything now was utterly compelling. There were no questions. Only responses. Every response was a passionate yes, a sensual, sighing, exultant, triumphant, soothing, satisfying yes, and ultimately an exhausted yes.

They lay in each other's arms, Thady slowly caressing away the aching inner glow of so much sustained excitement, soothing her into blissful relaxation. Then they slept, stirred and aroused the desire to make love again, to live once more in each other, and again their bodies tuned to a harmony that neither wanted to end.

There were times when Anne woke and wondered if this was a dream, but she had only to touch Thady and she was once more submerged in the warm and wonderful reality of him.

They did not talk. Implicit in every kiss and caress was an acceptance of each other that transcended words, and that acceptance erased all the loneliness they had known.

For now.

And that was all that mattered throughout this night of sharing.

CHAPTER TEN

ANNE WOKE TO LIGHT. The early morning sun was streaking the horizon with fingers of pink and gold. The water of the harbour was a pale glitter waiting for the deep azure blue of the day sky to soak in its colour.

Anne didn't feel tired, although she should have. The broken and intermittent night of sleep should have left her feeling exhausted; instead she felt more vibrantly alive than anytime in her life.

Thady lay behind her, one arm serving as a pillow for her head, the other holding her close to him, his hand resting lightly on her breast. She wriggled her toes against the top of his feet, felt his leg slide sensually over her own, rubbing against the softness of her thighs.

She felt Thady stir, knew that he was awake beside her, looking through the window at what was undoubtedly one of the most beautiful vistas in the world.

"A new day," she murmured, more to herself than to him.

His hand curled possessively around her breast and his leg trapped hers more firmly, his body instinctively asserting its hold on her as he answered, "A new life."

The past was done with, Anne thought exultantly. This *was* the beginning of a new life for them. Together. "What are you going to do today, Thady?" she asked, smiling, knowing what his reply would be.

He didn't answer straight away, but that didn't fray Anne's confidence. The way he was holding her was answer enough that he had no intention of letting her go anywhere without him. She snuggled her bottom and back more firmly against him, revelling in the security that his strong possessiveness imparted.

She thought of all that had happened in the past nine hours. Until last night, her experience of lovemaking was extremely limited. She had thought of it mainly as two bodies coming together, driven by biological urges. That was how she had felt it to be with Tom Colby. Now she understood that making love was an art form of intimacy and bonding and sharing, an intimacy so deep that once experienced would never let people pull apart.

"Today," said Thady, "I'm cancelling my flight to London. I'll wait and help you get ready to leave with me. We'll go together. If that suits you."

Anne's smile grew more serene. She had known it couldn't be any other way. Not after last night. "I couldn't think of anything better," she said.

"Do you feel hungry?"

"Ravenous."

"I'll order breakfast."

He rolled away from her to pick up the telephone. Anne turned, compelled to keep him in sight, in touch. She ran her hand lightly over the firm muscles of his shoulders and back. He had a beautiful physique. She loved the lines of his taut, cheeky bottom. Somehow it was the perfect contrast to the strength of his upper body and the virile power of his thighs.

She drew tantalising little patterns with her fingertips, mischievously enjoying Thady's reactions as he tried to give the breakfast order.

The receiver crashed down. Thady spun to Anne, caught her hands and pinned them down, leaning over her, playing the role of dominant male. Except that the green eyes were dancing with pleasure from her teasing.

"You are a very wicked woman," he declared, his voice unashamedly lacking in censure.

"Let he who is free from defects, cast the first stone," she retorted archly.

He laughed, his whole face illuminated with inner joy. Anne had always thought him handsome, but in that moment it seemed to her that Thady Riordan had to be the most beautiful man in the world. She felt her heart turn over.

"I think I need a shave," he said, releasing one of her hands to feel the stubble around his jaw. "Yes, definitely a shave." The green eyes twinkled with sheer devilment as his mouth moved into a tantalising curve. "I wouldn't want to put you off because I wasn't as perfect for you as I can possibly be."

He bounded off the bed and strode across the room to where he had dropped his bathrobe the night before. Anne hitched herself up on the pillows to watch him. He moved with an arrogant grace that reminded her very forcefully of how he had orchestrated all that had happened from the time he had first accepted what she wanted with him.

For one stomach-churning moment Anne wondered how many women had known him like this. Then she determinedly squashed the thought. He had told her all those other women had been meaningless to him. He had come back to Australia for her because she was special to him. He cared about her. So this was different. They were lovers in the true sense of the word. After last night, it couldn't be anything else.

He picked up the bathrobe and pulled it on. He gathered up her clothes from the floor near the window. He was turning toward her when something made him pause. She saw him frown at one of the armchairs. Then he leaned over and picked up the little gold box she had tossed away as something she didn't want from him.

"You didn't open my gift to you." He brought it to her, an indulgent smile on his lips, a sparkle of anticipation in his eyes. "You have no excuse not to accept it now."

She flashed him a smile of courteous curiosity and started pulling apart the fancy ribbon bow, teasing Thady with a show of nonchalance. She would, of course, express delight and surprise and wonder at his marvellous gift when she got to it. But in reality, whatever the gift was, it was irrelevant now. Thady had given himself to her. That was the only gift that was important.

She unwrapped the gold paper and found a black velvet box. Jewellery, she thought. Men always gave jewellery to their women. It was probably part of their genetic pattern. Still maintaining an outward air of nonchalance, Anne sprang the catch and opened the lid.

She froze with shock when she saw what lay within. Into her stunned mind slid Thady's words of yesterday. *Years from now you might look at something I gave you and remember me kindly.*

Her heart clenched painfully at the cruelty of his kindness. Not that she thought Thady meant to be cruel, but such a gift made certain that the giver would be totally unforgettable. Such a gift would keep the memory of him alive forever. Impossible for any other man of Anne's acquaintance to match it.

She managed to tear her eyes from what had to be worth a king's ransom. There was something almost obscene about the extravagance of this gesture from him. It had to be wrong. Grossly wrong. She swung her head violently from side to side. "No, Thady. It's too much. You shouldn't have done this."

He sat down beside her. He cupped her face in his hands to still her nervous agitation. The green eyes bored through the emotional confusion in hers, blazing their own conviction of what was right to him and searing away any need to object to his generosity.

"I want to see them on you, Anne. I want to see if they suit you. I had them specially designed for you at De Mestres in Brussels. Please put them on."

Specially designed for her before he came back to Australia to press his claim on her. Was this how he handled his relationships with women, buying them designer jewellery beforehand? Anne swallowed to clear the tightness from her throat. She fought to keep the pain out of her eyes as she questioned his intentions.

"You meant to use them? To persuade me?"

"No." He frowned and shook his head in decisive denial. "They were for you. No matter what happened between us."

He had already proved that, Anne reminded herself. Yet her heart still recoiled from accepting them as she stared down at the perfectly matched diamond earrings. They were designed as small flowers, yet the diamonds in the petals were larger than the diamond in Jenny's engagement ring, and the centre stone of each earring was far larger than any she had ever seen, utterly dazzling in their clarity and brilliance.

It was the kind of gift that a man gave to a highly prized mistress, and she would have given anything for the box to have contained a simple little ring that promised a lifelong commitment. Despite having accepted that their relationship was not to be on those terms, it still hurt to think that Thady would never ask her to be his wife. All the more so after last night. Yet she had promised not to try to change the kind of man he was.

"Don't you like them?" Thady asked, concern and disappointment threading through the soft caring in his voice.

"Of course I do. Who wouldn't? They're the most fabulous earrings I've ever seen," Anne replied truthfully, yet still she didn't want to accept them.

"Then please put them on, Anne."

Denying him this would only stir rejection between them, Anne argued to herself. The desire to please him, to be in harmony with him again overrode her deep-seated reservations. She lay the box on the bed and with nervously fumbling fingers removed the gold studs she had put in her earlobes yesterday. She set them on the bedside table, then turned her attention to Thady's gift, conscious of him watching and waiting for her to complete his bidding.

She forced herself to meet his eyes as she fastened first one, then the other earring to her lobes. She saw twinkling anticipation glow into intense satisfaction when she finally lowered her hands. His gaze roved slowly over her face, down her throat to the tangled mass of her hair falling over her shoulders, then to her breasts still bared for his pleasure.

Anne felt her nipples stiffen. She couldn't help it. What Thady was thinking was clearly written on his face: *My woman.* While into her mind crept the awful thought, *Bought and paid for.*

"You look so beautiful," he murmured huskily.

She forced a bright smile. "I'm glad you think so."

He laughed, his face aglow with happy satisfaction. "Come. I'll show you," he said, rising to his feet and taking her hands to pull her up with him.

He led her to a mirror and stood behind her, trailing his fingers through her hair to fan it out away from her ears. The diamond flowers flashed with a myriad facets of glittering light, making her look a very expensive and classy lady, even in her naked and unkempt state.

"They're perfect for you," Thady said in decisive triumph. "And you enhance them."

The material and unimportant things in life, Anne thought, and felt relief when a knock on the door saved her from having to find an appropriate answer.

"That will be breakfast," Thady said, turning away to open the door. "There's another robe in the bathroom."

Anne took temporary refuge in the bathroom, suddenly hating the situation she was in. It was not only the suite's butler coming in, seeing that Thady Riordan had a woman with him. The diamond earrings somehow made the whole scene unsavoury. They seemed to scream that she and Thady were not equal lovers.

She could accept that there was to be no marriage, but she couldn't accept him giving her more than she could give him. It had to be a complementary relationship, with respect on both sides. She couldn't bear it to be any other way.

Anne washed and tidied up her appearance as best she could, wishing she could tear off the diamonds but knowing she couldn't yet. It would raise questions she didn't want to answer. Later on she could say they didn't suit the clothes she had to put on to leave the hotel.

Other excuses ran through her mind. They were to be reserved for a special occasion. She didn't know what that occasion would be, but she knew intuitively that if it didn't arise, she would never wear the diamond flowers again. Thady might feel right about them, but she didn't, and while she didn't want to hurt Thady by rejecting the gift he had specially chosen for her, until she could feel right about it, the earrings would remain in the black velvet box.

Breakfast was all set out for her when she emerged from the bathroom. The butler had been dismissed and Thady obviously took pleasure in seeing that Anne was served with everything she wanted. It was easy to relax and enjoy their new togetherness. Their awareness of each other seemed to sharpen their appetites, making everything taste better than it ever had before.

They discussed how to settle Anne's commitments in Australia. There was packing to be done, the terrace house to be put into the hands of an agent for subletting, personal effects to be put into storage or left with her mother or Jenny.

Apart from settling her own business, Anne also had to organise the dressmaking for Jenny's wedding before she left. A promise was a promise, and Anne was not about to let her youngest sister down.

There were also telephone calls to be made, informing people of her departure from the country, not only to business connections, but family and friends. All in all, Anne figured she could be ready to leave by the end of the week.

In that calculation she completely underestimated the driving force that Thady brought to bear on the situation. Having taken on a new life, he lived it to the full, driven by a seemingly inexhaustable passion to eke the most out of every moment. Not only was he an exciting, creative and inventive lover, he also threw himself into being totally supportive and caring of Anne's needs. It took only three days to finalise all her preparations for her departure to England with Thady.

So accustomed was she to doing everything for herself, Anne felt oddly swamped by Thady's constant attention and consideration for her. Their relationship was so different from what she had experienced with Tom Colby. Far more intense, far more intimate.

She had the feeling of not being herself any more. She learnt an entirely new appreciation of the word "couple." She didn't move or think or feel without Thady being an inextricable part of the moving and thinking and feeling. It both exhilarated and frightened her. Having had nothing from him for so long, it now seemed that so much couldn't possibly last.

This underlying fear made her cautious in her conversation with Jenny when they went to the dressmaker with the designs for the wedding.

"Being with Thady Riordan is right for you, isn't it, Anne?" Jenny pressed, her bright brown eyes dancing with pleasure. "You're positively glowing, so it has to be right."

"For the present," Anne conceded. "But since I don't know how the future will work out with Thady, I'd prefer the rest of the family to view my going to England as a career move. Nothing more, Jenny."

This warning evoked a more worried look. "I hope I didn't... He *will* marry you when he gets used to the idea, won't he, Anne?"

"Jenny, it's my life. My decision," Anne assured her gently. "Whatever happens is not your responsibility. I just don't want Mum reading something more than there is into the situation. You know how she goes on and on about getting married."

"You can't hide it forever, Anne. Besides, I bet it's only a matter of time before Thady decides he wants you as his wife," Jenny declared with all the confidence of her youth and experience. "With you doing the production design for his plays, the two of you have to be perfect for each other."

It felt that way, Anne thought, but although Thady's actions and his manner towards her spoke of a deep and compelling need for her, he hadn't once spoken of love.

Jenny, however, held to her own opinion about how matters stood. When she drove Anne to the terrace house in Paddington where Thady was organising the packing of her reference books, she made her stand on the point of family.

"I'll be dreadfully disappointed if Anne can't make it to my wedding," she informed Thady, using her big eyes to their best imploring effect. "It's just before Christmas, you know."

"Yes. Anne told me," Thady said quietly.

"You must take a break for Christmas," Jenny prompted.

"Always." For a moment there was something dark and haunted in the deep green eyes. Then he gave Jenny an indulgent smile. "Don't worry, Jenny. I'll make sure that Anne comes home for your wedding. And for Christmas."

Jenny threw Anne a triumphant grin as though that settled the family question for good and all.

Anne was not quite so certain, but she decided not to question what the brief glimpse of pain in Thady's eyes had meant. She imagined that past Christmases had been times of intense loneliness for him, and she silently vowed that this coming Christmas would be very different for him if she had anything to do with it.

The moment the front door closed on her sister, Thady swept Anne into his arms and kissed her with a storming passion that expressed an urgent need to affirm what they had together—or a need to blot out something else. They ended up making love amidst the packing cases, and the wildly erotic excitement of that coupling pushed every other thought out of Anne's mind for some considerable time. It was much later that she wondered whether it had been the talk of a wedding or Christmas that had stirred Thady into taking her as he had.

There was so much to learn about him, yet some intuitive sense warned her that she would only raise barriers between them if she tried probing into the hidden depths of Thady Riordan. Their sharing was restricted to the immediate. And the future. She could only hope that would eventually change as their relationship forged a deeper confidence between them.

Perhaps it was the coward's way out, but Anne employed the telephone to communicate her news and make her farewells to her mother and her two other sisters before departing for England. All of them complained about not having the chance to see her before she went. Anne insisted there was no time and she would see them all at Jenny's wedding.

The truth was she did not want her relationship with Thady subjected to her family's curiosity. It was far too new and private. She would write to them from London and gently lead into her real position with him. Not that she expected her mother to ever approve of an unconventional living arrangement, but the ground had to be prepared for Thady's eventual appearance at her side. She hoped that by giving her mother time to get used to the idea, Leonie Tolliver might come to accept it gracefully.

Anne realised she wasn't quite used to the idea herself, particularly when they arrived at Mascot Airport on Thursday morning and Thady went about the business of booking their luggage onto their flight to London, automatically coupling her with himself.

She had no regrets about putting her life and well-being into his hands, but she was nervously conscious of having burnt all her bridges behind her when they went through the last gate to board the Qantas Boeing jet. A steward settled them into their first-class seats and served them glasses of champagne. Thady tipped his glass to hers in a private toast, and his smile settled some of the flutters in her stomach.

This is like being married and going off on a honeymoon, Anne thought. Women throughout all of history have faced this situation. They fall in love, then go off with their men to start a different life and make a family of their own together. There was nothing new in what she was doing. It was exciting, challenging and no cause at all for the absurd well of tears that was pricking at her eyes. She sipped her champagne, determined to face her future with Thady in a happy frame of mind.

"Miss Tolliver, Mr. Riordan, can I refill your glasses?"

The steward hovered over them, not realising he had spoken the ultimate truth. Annelise Tolliver was not married. She was Thady Riordan's new live-in lover. She would never be married to him. He had made that perfectly clear. The photo of her wedding day would never appear on her mother's mantel along with her other sisters'. She would never have a family.

Anne hurriedly repressed these defeatist thoughts. She had given Thady her word that she would not try to change him, but that didn't mean he could not change himself. He had never been with her before.

Not like this. Not with such wonderfully exclusive togetherness.

The jet engines began to thrum. The huge plane taxied into position on the runway for take off. Thady smiled at her and took her hand in his, squeezing it gently as they were lifted into the air en route to the other side of the world.

His eyes warmly reflected her thoughts—the start of a new life. Anne privately added another—the end of loneliness.

CHAPTER ELEVEN

LONDON SURPRISED ANNE when they arrived twenty-two hours later feeling tired and rather ragged. The city was more squat than she had imagined. She quickly realised its charm and character lay in its time-honoured and traditional architecture. Faceless sky-scrapers had no historical soul.

The day was bitterly cold and grey. Soft intermittent showers followed their taxi all the way from Heathrow to Knightsbridge. If this was autumn in England, what was winter going to be like? Certainly she would need to buy much warmer clothes.

The taxi came to a halt in front of an impressive brick building, four storeys high and featuring lots of lovely bay windows. Whenever the sun did shine in London, Anne imagined it streaming through them, and she felt her heart lighten at making her home here. Their luggage was transferred to a central lift, and Thady pressed the button for the top floor.

The lift opened to what seemed like a private foyer, since only one double set of doors led off from it. Anne threw an inquiring look at Thady, who was busily emptying the lift of bags and suitcases.

"Use the key I gave you," he instructed matter-of-factly.

"This flat takes up the whole floor?" she asked.

"Yes."

Anne unlocked the door with an odd feeling of trepidation, aware that such a spacious flat had to cost the earth as it was situated in virtually the centre of London. She realised the moment she set foot inside that it was very definitely someone's home. Someone's extremely luxurious home.

Thady's possession of the key he had given her meant he had access to it. Did it belong to a friend who had gone abroad for two years? Certainly there was a great deal of trust involved, since there had been no attempt to store the personal possessions that gave the place its character.

"How did this flat come to be available to you, Thady?" Anne asked wonderingly.

She was so busy taking in the features of the huge living room that she didn't immediately notice Thady's lack of reply. Music obviously played a large part in the owner's life, she thought. A highly polished black grand piano graced one corner. At the far end of the room stood two tall black speakers for whatever sound system was stored in a massive wall unit of glassed bookcases and closed cupboards.

The carpet was a deep maroon. Black leather sofas were grouped around a large square marble coffee table. The marble had a rose hue but was strongly veined in grey and black. There were curious pieces of abstract sculpture that somehow emitted an invitation to touch and feel. The paintings on the walls were abstracts, as well, but they suggested a far more complex visual experience, layers and layers of brooding meaning.

As the mood of the room seeped into Anne, pressing an awareness of sensuality and dark passions and lonely pleasures, she had no need for Thady to answer her question. She spun around to face him and found him watching her, waiting to evaluate her response to this extension of himself.

"This is *your* home," she said quietly.

"I've lived here for some years," he subtly corrected her. His mouth took on a wry curve. "I would have removed my personal effects before you came, Anne. I can easily do so if and when you prefer not to live with me."

"Why?" she asked, her eyes challenging the apparent carelessness behind his words. She lifted her hands in helpless bewilderment. "Why give up all this to let me stay?"

He shrugged. "You need a base in London. I don't."

"But where would you have gone if I'd taken up what you offered me?"

"Away from here. Ireland. America. It wouldn't have mattered. When I'm writing there is nothing else that exists for me."

Anne felt a chill run down her spine. Would he shut her out when he began to write again? What kind of life together would they have then?

"Having you makes everything different, Anne," he said softly.

He moved forward and wrapped her in his arms. His warm hands took the chill away. His warm mouth claimed hers with a passion that suggested he was well content to lose himself in her, wanting nothing else to exist but the intense physical and emotional intimacy that came with making love together.

The unpacking was left until later.

Thady's bedroom was done in shades of green, a rich room of silk and satin and velvet with darkly gleaming rosewood furniture. The ensuite bathroom was equally luxurious, featuring a Jacuzzi set in green onyx and gold fitments adorning every other convenience. Anne became very familiar with both rooms during her first weekend in London. Thady definitely had his own unique ideas about how best to overcome jet lag. Apart from which, the weather was not conducive to sightseeing.

There was plenty of food in the well-appointed kitchen, and they made snacks for themselves whenever they felt hungry. Thady explained that a housekeeper came in weekdays to look after day-to-day maintenance.

He designated one of the spare bedrooms for Anne to use as a workroom. She could use a second bedroom, as well, if she needed more space.

He had turned another room into a study for himself. It was there that Anne secluded herself to read his new play while Thady listened to music in the living room. Somehow it did not surprise her when she heard Wagner's opera *Götterdämmerung* being played. The dark, sweeping grandeur of ''The Twilight of the

Gods'' was very much in keeping with the mood of what Thady had written.

It was a strong drama, weaving inexorably towards a conflagration of passions that would ignite any theatre. Thady had titled it *The Long Cold Winter,* but it was far from cold. Each scene throbbed with an underlying sexual tension that gradually drew every character out of their ego-image roles, finally building to a climax of explosive power that shattered every image and revealed the people underneath in all their lonely vulnerability.

It was undoubtedly the most gripping play Thady had written so far, and it was the simmering sexual element that made it so. Anne knew that what Thady wrote reflected his own inner world. She could not help wondering if he had accepted her need for him because of his desire for the release and full expression of his strong sexuality.

She remembered that awful afternoon with Jenny when she had begged him not to go and he had bluntly told her he could not repress his physical feelings. She remembered the desire and purpose emanating from him at their initial meeting at the Park Hyatt, enfolding her, tying her to him. And from the night she had gone to him, it was as though his need for sexual expression was not only intense but wellnigh insatiable.

He had told her.

Warned her.

Shown her.

He had done his utmost, denied himself in order not to hurt her. She was not going to be hurt now because his need for her was predominantly physical.

She did not hear the music stop. She did not hear Thady enter the study or come up behind the leather armchair where she had curled up to read his play. The first she knew of his presence was the touch of his hands on her shoulders, hands that slid slowly down to caress her breasts as he leant over the backrest and grazed his lips across her hair.

"Finished?" he murmured.

Her heart thumped a painful protest at the response her body instinctively gave him. "Yes," she whispered, her breath catching in her throat as desire for him overwhelmed all other considerations.

"I was waiting for you to come and give me your opinion on it," he said questioningly. "You've been in here a long time." She heard the rueful smile in his voice as he added, "I was beginning to wonder if that meant it was good or bad."

"You know it's good, Thady. Everyone who's read it will have told you it's going to be a sensational hit."

"Mmm..." He pressed a longer, warmer kiss on the top of her head. "So what have you been thinking?"

"How glad I am to be here with you."

She turned her head to smile at him. He gave a low, sexy growl and lifted her out of the chair, swinging her into full contact with him, then teasingly rolling her body against his.

"Now tell me the truth," he insisted, his eyes feasting off the response in hers. "Can you visualise it on stage yet?"

"Enough to start trying out ideas."

He gave her a wicked grin. "Let's go to bed and embellish them. We'll start the ball rolling tomorrow."

It wasn't all sex with Thady. They talked about aspects of the production design for his play long into the night. The mind sharing made the intimacy of their lovemaking all the more pleasurable. Anne was deeply happy to be his woman, whatever that meant to him.

On Monday morning Thady was all business, sweeping Anne off to Gray's Inn for a meeting with his solicitor, Paula Wentworth. He wanted the contract between them legally settled before taking Anne on to other important meetings.

Paula was a tall, slim woman who exuded professionalism from her neatly piled red hair to her low-heeled court shoes. Her skin was fine and very white, her eyes a sharply intelligent grey-green, her fine-boned face too long and narrow to be called pretty, yet there was a haughty elegance about her.

Thady greeted her with warmth, and it was obvious from the ensuing conversation that he had a long-standing association with Paula and her husband. Their manner to each other had the ease of close friendship, which surprised Anne. It suggested that Thady was not quite the loner she had imagined him to be.

Paula's manner to Anne conveyed a friendly interest, but there was a fast and keen measuring in her eyes that implied an intense curiosity about both Anne and the forceful impression she had apparently made on Thady Riordan. Thady's sudden and urgent insistence on such a blanket contract involving his work had obviously raised questions that had not been answered to Paula's satisfaction.

Paula went through the contract with them, altering a few details that had been on the faxed copy but that no longer applied now that Anne was in England. "Do you have an address in London yet?" she asked, raising her eyebrows at Anne in a sympathetic fashion, clearly expecting to hear the name of a stop-gap hotel.

Anne gave the address of the flat in Knightsbridge.

"Oh!" Paula swiftly covered her surprise with an understanding smile. "You're staying with Thady until—"

"No, Paula," Thady cut in quietly. "That is Anne's address in London until further notice."

This firm assertion evoked a quizzical frown. "You're moving out, Thady?"

"No," he answered. "Not in the foreseeable future."

Paula kept looking at him as though she couldn't quite believe what she was hearing. Thady returned her gaze without blinking an eyelid. The naked shock on the solicitor's face remained undisguised for several seconds. Then the grey-green eyes snapped into sharp reappraisal, searching, wondering, speculating.

Paula's lips sealed into a thin line that denoted a determination to be discreet. She forced her attention to the contract. From that moment on, nothing of a personal nature was said. It was strict concentration on business.

Every time Paula lifted her eyes to Anne, however, their quizzical look was far too intense for settling a legal point.

Several times Anne felt that the question in Paula's eyes was not, *Why you?* but, *Do you know what you've taken on?*

When all the legalities were approved and signed, Paula escorted them out of her office. "You and Anne must come to dinner soon," she said to Thady, then swept a smile at Anne. "My husband, Richard, will be delighted to meet you, Anne. He loves the theatre as much as I do."

Thady slid his arm around Anne's shoulders in what felt like both a protective and possessive gesture as he replied for both of them. "If you don't mind, Paula, we'll leave socialising for a month or two. We haven't had much time to ourselves as yet, and Anne is going to be very busy on the production design for the play."

"Of course," Paula conceded with easy charm. Then with an affectionate touch on Thady's arm, she added, "I hope this will be a very happy and productive association for both of you."

The sentiment was clearly genuine, yet Anne still sensed some deep reservation, perhaps even resentment in the other woman. As soon as they were out of the building she turned to Thady, her eyes probing his for understanding.

"Why was Paula Wentworth so shocked by us and what you've done for me? It's not as though you haven't had other women associated with you."

His mouth curved with a touch of self-mockery. "None like you, Anne."

"What do you mean, like me?"

"I'm not in the habit of having live-in relationships. Paula knows that since she first met me, no woman has ever got close to me in any intimate sense."

"But you said . . ."

"One can have sex without intimacy, Anne. It was not something I wanted for long with any one woman."

"How long?"

"An hour or two that left me feeling empty and unsatisfied and chillingly alone," he answered, his mouth curling with contempt for the need that had driven him into the beds of women he had no feeling for beyond a passing physical desire.

He drew her into his arms, uncaring of the curious looks of passers-by. A reckless and ruthless determination flitted over his face, and once again Anne felt he was defying some private demon in taking her into his life. The green eyes glittered with intense possessiveness.

He lifted a hand to her face, gently stroked her cheek, tilted her chin. "You know it's different with you, Anne. So different that the thought of it ending makes me want to have all I can of you while I can."

His mouth claimed hers in a long, devouring kiss. The staid and respectable establishments around them ceased to exist. Only their passion for each other had any reality until Thady reluctantly withdrew his mouth from hers.

Desire still simmered in his eyes as he gave her a crooked little smile. "Business before pleasure. As much as I'd like to take you home and ravish all your senses, we have an appointment with my director, who will not be impressed by unpunctuality."

He hailed a passing taxi and helped Anne into it. His hand curled tightly around hers as they relaxed on the back seat together. It was a link of intimacy that Anne found very reassuring.

She no longer had any doubt that she was uniquely special to him compared to all the other women he had known. Paula Wentworth's shocked surprise was confirmation enough that Thady had spoken the truth in his replies to her questions. Yet there was something in Thady that didn't look for a long and lasting future for their relationship.

Was it some deep and innate pessimism that dictated it could be snatched away from him at any moment? Or did he know something she didn't, something that compelled him to live for the moment and not look too far ahead? Did he have some hereditary illness in his family, something that would claim him at a relatively early age? Or perhaps he carried some hidden defect that made having children impossible or inadvisable.

"Thady?"

He turned to her, his eyes warmly caressing. Some-how the look of happy contentment on his face made Anne swallow the impulsive question that had leapt to her tongue. Did she want to know the worst that could happen to them? Might it not be better to leave every-thing as it was?

She squeezed his hand and smiled. "Is everyone going to have the same reaction to us as Paula Went-worth did?"

He laughed and lifted her hand to brush his lips over her knuckles. "Will you mind if they do?" he asked teasingly.

"Why should I mind being seen as the remarkable woman who got the ungettable man?" she answered loftily.

The wicked twinkle in his eyes was swallowed by a surge of dark turbulence. "Anne... There will come a time when I can't fulfil all your needs," he warned seriously. "I want you to feel free to walk away from me when that happens. I don't want you to feel tied or obligated to a relationship that isn't satisfying you."

"Why do you think that will happen, Thady?" she asked quietly.

He shook his head, and she could see his face clos-ing over his thoughts as he turned his head away from her. He heaved a deep sigh before tempering it with a surface smile. "I'm selfish enough to hope it won't. But I do mean that, Anne. You're free to do whatever you want. I'll never stand in your way."

Anne remembered reading somewhere that if you love someone you let them go free. She wanted to think that this was a gift of love from Thady to her, yet she could not shake off the feeling there was some other factor behind his words.

Whatever it was—if there *was* anything—Anne knew intuitively that Thady had made up his mind to keep it to himself. Whether that was to protect her, or protect what they had together as long as he could, Anne could not even guess. She told herself to be content with the one important thing that Thady had implied. *He* was not thinking of walking away from *her.* He was handing that decision to her.

Anne knew it was a decision she would never make. For better or for worse, she was tied to Thady Riordan in the deepest sense there could be between a man and a woman. She wanted to spend the rest of her life with him. As far as she was concerned, there *was* a marriage ring on her finger. She didn't need a band of gold to proclaim that truth.

CHAPTER TWELVE

FOR ANNE, the next two months were the most exciting, most challenging, most satisfying period of her life. She felt extended in a way she had never experienced before, working with people who demanded and expected the absolute best, mixing with people at a social level that took the best for granted.

At times Anne needed to be on her own to concentrate on developing her ideas for the production design of his play. Apart from that, Thady was always with her. He accompanied her to the theatre when work began there. He smoothed her path in a thousand ways, from lining up the contacts she needed to lending his strong support on any contentious issues that arose.

Thady Riordan left no-one in any doubt that he and Annelise Tolliver were in solid partnership where *The Long Cold Winter* was concerned, thereby giving Anne an acceptability, an authority and an automatic respect that would have been difficult to achieve on her own. Their personal relationship was never left in doubt, either. To many highly interested observers, they made the concept of *togetherness* a new art form.

One of those who actively displayed an intrigued curiosity was Alex Korbett, Anne's former boss. Alex had moved to England two years previously and was working on production designs for the English National Opera and the Royal Shakespeare Company. As soon as he heard of Anne's arrival in London and how intimately she was connected to Thady Riordan, Alex got in touch with them and offered any practical help Anne might require.

Alex was the only person in the country who knew of the previous association between Anne and Thady. For all his tendency to gossip, however, he never mentioned a word about it. While Anne marvelled at his restraint, she was also relieved. Thady was such a deeply private person that Anne was quite certain he appreciated any restraint that limited the flames of speculation already leaping around them.

Alex was as good as his word at giving Anne his assistance whenever it was needed. Anne suspected he secretly enjoyed knowing more than anyone else, and he took every opportunity to increase his understanding of the situation.

When Thady and Anne accepted a dinner invitation from Paula and Richard Wentworth, Alex was a fellow guest.

He was a rotund, affable little man, much in demand at parties for his quick wit and ready store of current gossip about people of interest. He lent a sparkle to the table conversation, Anne thought, but she found his shrewd perception of people somewhat disturbing. Later in the evening when they retired to the lounge for after-dinner coffee, she became even more disturbed.

While Paula claimed Thady's attention, Alex drew Anne aside, claiming her private attention. He led her to a sofa somewhat apart from the other guests. His sharp blue eyes noted her reluctance to be parted from Thady, and his opening remark was aimed at focussing her concentration entirely on himself.

"Anne, why isn't Thady writing anymore?"

Anne was bewildered by the question. The answer was so obvious to her. "You know we're involved in the production of *The Long Cold Winter*, Alex. Why would Thady be writing at this time?"

"Because he always has in the past."

Alex's reply jolted Anne, and sent an odd little shiver down her spine. Thady had said in Sydney that he had to get back to his writing. That he had not done so she put down to her sharing his life and home, and his absorption in her designs. His interest in the production she assumed as natural.

She frowned as she tried to re-evaluate the situation. "You mean he's never involved himself with production before?"

"Never," Alex replied decisively.

"But all the problems that come up—"

"A matter of total disinterest to him. 'You've got what I've written,' he'd say. 'Ruin it however you please. You'll never get out of it what I put into it.' And that, my dear Annelise, is a direct quote."

Alex's clever mimic of Thady's voice lent a chilling authenticity to the contemptuous words. This was an aspect of Thady's character Anne had never seen. She sensed more than knew his strength of will, recognised rather than experienced what she suspected to be the ruthless driving nature of the man.

He had shown her that capability within him in cutting off their relationship when he had judged it to be in her best interests, but apart from that, he had been good to her, helpful, benevolent, charming. As lover, comforter, companion and friend, she could ask no more of any man.

It was hard to accept that Thady could be so dismissive of his own work, especially since all his plays were recognised as masterpieces of the theatre. Yet according to Alex, and Anne could not disbelieve him, Thady was now acting entirely out of character. He had changed for her. Or she had changed him.

A heavy load of responsibility came down upon her shoulders. No wonder they were both a never-ending source of comment and speculation. *What am I doing to him? Why has he involved himself in production for the first time? Why has he involved himself with me?*

Anne looked around, needing to see him. She found him sitting with Paula at the other end of the room, but he was not looking at the other woman. He was looking directly at Anne, a heavy frown darkening his eyes. Paula said something to him, put her hand on his arm to draw his attention. He did not notice. His eyes were locked on Anne's, and the rest of the world was excluded from their contact.

Alex spoke to her in a low, urgent voice. "Anne, I can see this has come as a shock to you, but you must do something to get Thady writing again. He can't stop now. He's the genius of his generation. He probably will be, if he's not already, the greatest playwright of the twentieth century. You've got to help him."

Anne felt the flutter in her heart, felt her head swirl with dizziness. It often happened in moments of stress, and it was something she had no control over. The last time it had occurred was outside Thady's suite at the Park Hyatt, when his invitation to lunch had already turned into something else.

It was not frightening because she knew what it was. Her doctor had diagnosed it as a vaso-vagal reflex. For a split second the blood supply to her brain would be interrupted and she would feel the world spin. Then everything would right itself and the whooshing sensation was gone. Recovery was always swift. It was a minor irritation in life, no more. Anne instinctively settled herself against the backrest of the sofa, not because she had to, but because it automatically gave her a feeling of security against the sensation of falling.

Thady's head snapped up, like an animal's on alert for danger. His frown deepened. The next instant he was on his feet, totally unaware of breaking Paula's light grasp on his arm.

Anne straightened from her brief slump, the momentary attack over. Alex, whose speech had trailed off as he observed something wrong with her, quickly pushed his point before Thady came within earshot. "For God's sake, Anne! Make Thady write again!"

Then Thady was dropping to his knees beside her, his hands gripping her elbows too tightly, his face stamped with a strange mixture of fear and concern. "Are you ill, Anne?" Even his voice was a strained rasp, as though her reply was of critical importance to him.

She smiled indulgently, warmed by his deep caring. "No. I'm all right, Thady."

"I saw it, Anne. I saw it in your eyes." It was like an accusation, demanding that she not deceive him.

"Everything's fine. Truly," she assured him, beginning to feel embarrassed by the unnecessary fuss. All other conversation in the room had died. They were the focus of startled attention.

Something infinitely dangerous flared into Thady's eyes. "Has Alex said anything to upset you?" He turned towards Alex, and the look he gave him promised a deep, bloody, vengeful murder. "What have you said?" he demanded through lips that barely moved.

Alex visibly blanched under the savagery of that threatening gaze. It was shocking, a totally disproportionate reaction to what had happened.

"Nothing!" Alex and Anne cried in unison.

"I swear it, Thady. Nothing!" Alex added for good measure, a shaken note in his voice.

Thady's head turned slowly to Anne. The green eyes fastened onto hers. "Then what happened?" he asked with quiet insistence, but his fingers were biting into her flesh so hard it hurt.

"Nothing, really..."

"Tell me!"

She didn't want to. She didn't know why. Something was terribly wrong here. The tension swirled with far too much emotion. Alex was wiping his palms as though they were sweaty. The heave of Thady's chest was somehow frightening.

"Tell me!" he repeated.

Anne knew she had to. It was the only thing that might defuse this weirdly explosive situation. Paula's social occasion was definitely being spoilt by Thady's self-absorbed behaviour. It was up to Anne to do something about it.

"A silly medical condition..." she started, shaking her head over the trivial nature of the problem.

"Go on!"

"For a tiny fraction of a second..."

"Yes?"

"I get a tiny interruption in the blood supply to my brain. It means nothing—"

"God... God... *God!*"

It was a beat of despair and desperation such as Anne had never heard before. Thady bowed his head as though fate had dealt him too many blows and he could not sustain any more. It made her go cold all over. She shivered violently.

This brought another wild surge of reaction from Thady. He moved with lightning speed, his arms going around her shoulders, under her thighs. He lifted her effortlessly to his chest as though she were weightless. He straightened up, standing erect and tall. She could feel the mad pumping of his heart, saw the deathlike pallor of his face, and understood nothing.

He turned towards the remaining guests, all of whom were staring at them with expressions that ranged from puzzlement and surprise to curiosity and anticipation. All, that was, except Paula Wentworth. Her hand covered her mouth in a gesture of absolute horror.

That reaction also seemed grossly out of proportion to Anne. Admittedly Thady's behaviour had disrupted any comfortable and congenial conclusion to Paula's dinner party, but surely such a sophisticated and clever woman knew how to smooth such awkwardness without being horrified.

Anne closed her eyes on the whole scene, feeling too helpless to cope with it. Nothing made sense to her.

"Anne is sick. I'm taking her home," Thady announced in a voice that brooked no opposition.

Anne could have truthfully said she had never been so well in her life, but she was not about to contradict Thady's statement. The last thing she wanted was another outburst of violent feeling from him. The sooner they were alone together, the sooner she might be able to sort this whole madness out.

"I can walk, Thady," she murmured to him, half-opening her eyes to assure him of that point.

"I'm carrying you," he said grimly.

Richard Wentworth escorted them to the door.

"I'm so sorry," Anne whispered to him, painfully conscious of the scene they were making.

"We're all sorry to see you...stricken," Richard answered courteously.

Brisk good evenings were exchanged.

Thady walked rapidly to their car, his breath coming in short, harsh gasps.

"I'm all right, Thady. Truly I am," Anne pleaded. "You can put me down."

He didn't seem to hear. When he had her safely settled in the front passenger seat, his only reply was, "I'm taking you home."

He was still panting from his exertions when he seated himself in the driver's seat. The journey home was a nightmare. Thady insisted on hearing every detail of what had happened to her physically, and then her whole medical history from the time she was born. He was so doubting about the vaso-vagal reflex that Anne offered to get a medical certificate from her doctor in Sydney to prove what she said was true. To her further discomfort, Thady accepted her offer.

He doesn't trust me, Anne thought.

Or perhaps it was doctors he didn't trust, she amended, remembering her concerns about his health. She wished she had the courage to ask Thady about *his* medical history, but she couldn't bring herself to open up any area of jeopardy or disharmony on their future together. She knew there wasn't anything seriously wrong with her. She didn't want there to be anything seriously wrong with Thady, either.

A tense silence pervaded the atmosphere in the car by the time they reached Knightsbridge. Before Thady switched off the ignition, he turned to Anne with hardbitten resolve etched on his face.

"I don't want you to meet, speak to or see Alex Korbett again," he said.

That extraordinary demand left Anne speechless for a moment. That Thady was capable of ruthlessly cutting off people she knew only too well, yet Alex had done nothing to deserve such treatment. With Alex's love of the theatre, it was only natural that he be concerned about Thady's future as a playwright.

"Why?" she asked.

"What was Alex speaking to you about tonight?"

"Does it matter?"

"Yes."

He was deadly serious, his eyes searing hers with intensity. Anne wondered if she should bring up the subject of his writing. But surely what Thady did or did not do was *his* choice. She had promised not to try to change him.

"Nothing really," she dismissed as casually as she could.

"Was he talking about me?" Thady persisted.

"No," she lied, and instantly felt uncomfortable with the lie.

"What was it about then?"

"Old times in Sydney."

Why had she started this untruth? The answer was frighteningly obvious. She didn't want to hurt Thady. Nor did she want their relationship changed in any way. Whether Thady sensed or saw the lie she did not know. Her heart leapt erratically as his eyes searched hers with acute suspicion.

"Give me your promise not to have anything more to do with Alex Korbett," he commanded harshly.

"He's an old friend, Thady," she cried in protest. "Why should I cut him dead?"

The green eyes glittered with a ferocity that was entirely ruthless. "Because I'm insanely jealous of him," Thady bit out, each word reinforced by the violent emotion he was clearly feeling.

Anne stared at him incredulously, knowing that now Thady was lying. He had no reason to be jealous of anyone, let alone Alex Korbett. Apart from which, she was certain that Thady was not the kind of man to be jealous without more than sufficient cause. He was essentially a fair man, a giving man.

What has become of us? she thought. *How have we come to this?* They were both lying over what should have been a trivial matter. Everything seemed to have been blown all out of proportion, mountains being made out of molehills.

"Give me your promise, Anne."

She shook her head. It was all wrong. Unreasonable. "I can't do that, Thady," she said quietly.

"Why not?"

"Because it's unfair to Alex."

"Unfair!" He snarled the word, then jerked his head aside, looking out at the night that surrounded them with its darkness. He gave a low bitter laugh, then fell into a silent brooding that grated more on Anne's nerves than the laugh had.

She could feel him separating himself from her, withdrawing. Panic seized her. The need to fight for what she wanted forced a wild spill of words.

"You said I was free to do whatever I wanted, Thady. Why are you putting restrictions on me now? I'm with you because I want to be. I worked with Alex for three years. You know there's nothing between him and me but friendship. What possible harm can there be to us if Alex and I—"

"Let me be the judge of that, Anne!" he whipped back at her, his eyes ablaze with fierce determination.

"Like you were the judge of walking out of my life for seven years?" she retorted.

His face tightened. A muscle in his cheek contracted. He spoke slowly but with forceful deliberation. "Whether you believe me or not, Alex Korbett can change things between us. If you *need* me in your life, Anne, I *need* that promise from you. Now. Without equivocation."

He meant it. Resolution rang in his voice. It was stamped on his face. It burned in his eyes, challenging the need for him that he had answered when she had asked.

Anne didn't like it. She didn't understand it. But *need* was a powerful word. Thady would not use it lightly. She knew there was far more to his demand than he was telling her. It was not jealousy. It was not possessiveness either. Nor did she believe it had anything to do with whether he was writing or not.

Something was being kept hidden from her, something that he would not reveal under any circumstance. Nor would she allow anyone else, like Alex or Paula, to reveal whatever it was that was so intensely private to him, whatever it was that could change things between them.

The threat of change was enough to sway her. She had to answer his need, no matter what the reason behind it. He was far more important to her than Alex Korbett, and what they shared was far too precious to risk on some point of friendship with another man.

"I promise," she said dully, wishing that they'd never gone to Paula Wentworth's dinner party.

Thady gave a deep sigh of relief, then leaned forward and switched off the ignition. They were home, but the thought gave Anne no comfort. A shadow of mistrust had entered their lives, tarnishing what had seemed perfect before tonight.

When Thady opened the passenger door for her and she stepped out, the darkness of the night seemed to pulse with secrets. Whatever had transpired at Paula's party was shut behind them, just as Thady shut the car door behind her. But the secrets were still there . . . waiting for another time and place.

Anne took a deep breath. Suddenly it seemed very important to live for the present. She simply didn't know what tomorrow might bring. She could no longer trust it to bring unshadowed happiness.

CHAPTER THIRTEEN

THADY WAS EVEN MORE attentive to Anne and her needs in the days that followed Paula Wentworth's dinner party. Anne could not help wondering if *he* thought time was running out for them. He seemed obsessed with keeping her in sight when he wasn't actually by her side.

The fax came from her medical practitioner in Sydney, reinforcing what she had told Thady about the vaso-vagal reflex and her general state of health. His constant vigilance eased off. While Thady continued to be with her more often than not, he was far more relaxed about their togetherness. Anne realised he had simply been on guard in case something happened to her. Not possessive. Protective.

If Anne had needed any proof that Thady was not of a jealous nature, it came unequivocally when Tom Colby was suddenly cast in the lead male role of *The Long Cold Winter*. The play had already been in rehearsal for three weeks when the actor originally cast for the part, a well-known star of the London stage, was seriously injured in a falling elevator. The naming of a relatively unknown Australian actor as his replacement caused a flurry of publicity.

It also came as a shock to Anne. She had lost touch with Tom years ago and had no idea that he was in England. When Thady broke the news to her, she couldn't take it in at first.

"How? Why?" she floundered, anxiously searching Thady's eyes for his reaction to having her former lover in the lead role in his play.

"He has the ability to do it as it should be done," Thady answered with calm authority. Then his eyes were searching hers. "Do you mind, Anne?"

"No...no, I'm glad for him. It's a big break for Tom. Maybe it will make up for..." She hastily swallowed the words she had been going to say, suddenly sensitive of speaking about the hurt she had given to another man.

"That's over for him, Anne," Thady said softly. "He's married to an English girl he met while playing repertory in the provinces."

Anne shook her head in bewilderment. "How do you know?"

"I met him six months ago. I went to Birmingham to see him act in my last play."

"Why?"

"I wanted to know how good he was." Thady's mouth curved with dry irony. "I also wanted to know if there was any chance of you joining him in England."

"What if you'd found there was a chance?" Anne asked curiously.

"Then there would have been no chance for me," he answered simply.

It gave Anne an eerie feeling that so much had been decided about her without her knowledge, without her having anything to do with it. She had a mental image of a set of scales being tipped this way and that, influencing the course of her life without any choosing by her. It was unnerving to think the balance she had achieved with Thady could be tipped again by secret factors that had unknown and immeasurable weight.

Like her health. Which was now cleared. But Thady's extreme concern about it had not been answered to her satisfaction. Even Paula Wentworth's excuse did not ring completely true. When Anne had called her to thank her for the dinner and apologise for the somewhat melodramatic scene, Paula had smoothed away any awkwardness.

"Everyone understands, Anne," she had lightly assured her. "Thady has been alone for so long, naturally the thought of losing you horrified him. You did look deathly pale, you know. I'm awfully glad, for both of you, that it's nothing serious."

Anne felt there was more to it than that. The question still remained. Why wouldn't Thady marry her? They were so happy together, made for each other, yet it was obvious that if there'd been any chance of Tom Colby marrying her, Thady would have stayed out of her life.

At least that issue was settled, Anne thought with considerable relief. It was even more thoroughly settled the next day when she and Thady met Tom Colby at rehearsal. There could be no doubt Tom knew of

Anne's relationship with Thady, but it was clear from the first moment that Tom considered his own affair with Anne completely dead and buried.

He greeted them both with obvious pleasure, congratulating Anne on the huge step up in her career and thanking Thady profusely for the chance he had been given. This deep and sincere gratitude seemed to extend to Anne, as though she had something to do with his luck in being chosen. His whole manner stirred Anne's curiosity enough to ask Thady about it as soon as the director called Tom away.

"Why was Tom thanking you, Thady?"

"I used my influence to get him the part over the other actors who were being considered."

For a moment Anne saw the gleam of ruthlessness in the green eyes, the drive that had made him what he was in the theatrical world. He had wanted Tom Colby to play the lead, and he had asserted his will and used his power to enforce it, regardless of what others thought. Yet, if what Alex Korbett had told her was true, Thady had never involved himself in anything like this before.

"Why?" she asked, wondering if Thady was testing her love in some way by bringing Tom in.

"To enhance your work, Anne," he answered quietly. "I've seen Tom Colby act. I know what he can do. I wanted the best for you."

She felt shamed by doubting his trust in her and deeply moved by his commitment to her success. Thady might not have given a damn about how his other plays had been presented to the public, but he cared about this one because it could make or break her name in production design. He had been with her all this time, overseeing everything entirely for *her* sake. He had even given up his writing to ensure *her* success.

Although Thady had never said he loved her, Anne was convinced that all he had given her *was* a gift of love. Their relationship was all she had dreamed of, yet still there was the spectre of impermanence hanging over it.

The invitation to Jenny's wedding arrived. They were going through the mail while they sipped pre-dinner drinks. Anne passed the card to Thady, smiling over Jenny's choice of bells and bows etched in gold. Thady's responding smile suddenly died as he glanced through the formal invitation. His gaze lifted slowly to Anne's, his eyes dark green and oddly opaque.

"I'm sorry if there's been some misunderstanding, Anne. I never go to weddings. And that includes Jenny's."

"But you said . . ." Anne's mouth dried at the flat rejection written on his face.

"I said I'd make sure you were there, Anne. And for Christmas with your family, as well. I've already booked your ticket home. Everything is in order, as I promised."

Anne's mind spun with shock. He had only bought *her* airline ticket! He meant her to go home on her own!

"I thought..." She felt as though an iron fist was closing around her heart. She had to force herself to continue speaking. "I thought you'd want to be with me, Thady."

"Anne..." A conflict of interests warred across his face as he saw the pain of his decision clearly written on hers. The next instant he was on his feet and drawing her into his embrace, soothing her hurt with a trail of warm kisses around her temples.

"Being with you is a happiness I never expected or hoped to have," he murmured huskily. "I'm sorry you're disappointed that I won't be going to Australia with you. It's impossible anyway. I have business in America."

"Then I'll come with you," she pressed, her eyes searching his for reassurance that this separation need not be.

His face closed against her appeal. "No. You promised your sister."

"Jenny will understand," she pleaded.

He dragged in a deep breath. His eyes darkened. He spoke in a tight, flat voice. "No. The answer can only be no. It must always be no whenever I go to America. I can only give you so much, Anne. There are things for which I need to be alone. I did warn you there would come a time when I couldn't fulfil all your needs. This is one of those times. I'll be with you until you fly out to Australia. My business in America is for me to do by myself. Please accept that."

Anne didn't want to, but Thady was leaving her no choice. Any argument about it would be futile. She could either accept what he did give her, or walk away. Walking away from Thady was unthinkable to Anne. Her mind frantically searched for some reason why he needed to be alone.

"Is it to do with your writing?"

His mouth twisted into a grimace. "Perhaps."

Anne didn't know what to think. Certainly he had not written anything since she had been with him. If she was a distracting influence, it wasn't fair of her to expect him to stay with her all the time.

"How long will you be away?" she asked anxiously.

His eyes took on a dull, faraway look. "There are no certainties in this life, Anne. Who knows what will happen in the meantime? But I plan to be back in London by the middle of January."

It was not the complete assurance Anne craved, but she instinctively hid her own uncertainties under a bright smile as she curled her arms around his neck and pressed her body to his. "Then I guess I'd better make the most of this time with you," she said invitingly.

She saw the flicker of relief in his eyes before his mouth came down on hers, demonstrably wanting all she gave him. Yet it wasn't enough. If he needed to be free of her in order to write, then this would be the first of many separations.

Later that night, when Thady lay asleep beside her, Anne fretted over the separation he was insisting upon. Thady had a bad habit of deciding for himself what was best for her. What if he didn't really mean to come back from America?

Her mind flitted back and forth over all they had shared together. Thady *was* happy with her. Happier than he had ever expected to be. He had acknowledged that. Yet there were those dark hidden areas inside him that he kept from her.

Maybe he had been suppressing his needs for her sake. He could be thinking that after the opening night of *The Long Cold Winter,* she would be assured of a long and successful career without him at her side. He might consider he had done all he could for her.

Perhaps it was his nature to give himself completely to whatever he was doing, shutting out everything else. He had undoubtedly chosen to give himself entirely to her until he went to America. When he gave the same kind of total intensity to his work, would that be like an exorcism of her from his life?

Thady had cut her out of his life before without a moment's notice. Why should it be different this time? She had spent most of the past seven years alone. She did not want to spend the rest of her life alone. There were so many uncertainties about the future with Thady that Anne could see only one solution to her problem. She agonised over it until the first light of morning was filtering through the bay window curtains. She remembered watching the sunrise on her first morning with Thady. *A new day,* she had murmured then. *A new life,* he had answered.

Ironically, it was that recollection that finally brought Anne to a firm decision. A new life it would be. If something happened so she could not be with the man she loved in the years ahead of her, she would have his child to love.

Which meant no more contraception. With any luck at all, she should become pregnant before she and Thady went their separate ways. It was almost three weeks to the opening night of the play, another four days after that before she flew out of London. There was time for her to conceive.

Then she remembered her concern that Thady might have some hereditary illness that precluded him from having healthy children. Should she risk it? He was in his thirties with no sign of anything wrong with his health. It was worth risking, Anne decided. Thady had already made too many choices for her. This was going to be *her* choice, without any consultation with him. Whatever the consequences, she would live with them.

The decision gave Anne a peace of mind that allowed her to live through the next few weeks without worrying about the future. She had a heady sense of recklessness, of freedom from all fear. For the first time in her life she felt in control of what was to happen to her, and her secret excitement about conceiving Thady's child enhanced the pleasure and happiness of being with him.

She loved him more dearly when they made love, her emotions more deeply involved with thinking of him as the father of the child she wanted. Afterwards she held on to him for a long time, wondering if this was the night that had seeded a new life.

She made no mention of their coming separation, or the future beyond that, but the intensity of her feeling was such that it led Thady into trying to reassure her that he would be coming back to her in the new year. A mellow tenderness crept into his lovemaking, a soft caring for her pleasure that was more like absolute loving.

It was a time of wonderful harmony between them, and Anne stored every moment of it in her memory. She told herself it was better to have a taste of perfection than never to have known it. When it ended, it ended. There was nothing she could do about that except what she was already doing.

Her only disagreement with Thady occurred on the opening night of the play. The premiere was to be a glittering affair, attended by the Princess of Wales and a list of other celebrities that would have awed Anne three months ago. As it was, she kept nervously checking her appearance in the mirror prior to leaving for the theatre.

"You look stunningly beautiful," Thady assured her.

Anne laughed self-consciously. "You're only saying that because you chose the dress."

It was a fabulous evening dress in deep red velvet. Anne would never have paid the price Thady had paid for it, but she had to admit she was glad he had insisted. The amber beading on the tight bodice gave the dress a rich medieval look that somehow suited her extremely well, emphasising the gold in her eyes and the honey colour of her hair, which had been looped into a confection of tiny braids and loose curls.

She was satisfied that she looked suitably elegant for the occasion, yet as Thady's partner, she was aware there would be many critical eyes on her. He, of course, looked stunningly handsome in formal dress, and was totally assured of his reception by everyone.

"You're dithering for no good purpose," Thady gently chided. "The only thing that would add perfection to perfection is if you change those garnet earrings for the diamonds I gave you when we were in Sydney."

"I don't think the diamonds would go with this dress, Thady," Anne quickly excused. "I wouldn't feel right in them."

The latter statement was the real truth. Perhaps it was some stupid form of superstition, but in her mind she equated the diamonds with being married to him, and somehow she felt if she ever wore them prematurely, Thady would never marry her. He might never marry her anyway. He was so much against marriage he wouldn't even go to weddings. But Anne could not stop herself from hoping that one day he might change his mind.

Thady frowned at her. "Why aren't they right, Anne? I thought diamonds went with anything, yet you always say they're not right. You haven't worn them since I gave them to you."

"I'd rather keep them for a special occasion," she rushed out unthinkingly.

"Isn't this a special occasion?"

He looked hurt at her refusal, and Anne inwardly squirmed in the hole she had dug for herself. "I meant a special time that was only for you and me," she said weakly. "Not for show to other people."

Thady looked as though he wanted to pursue the point, but then changed his mind and shrugged it away, much to Anne's relief. He glanced at his watch and declared that her dithering time was up.

As she accompanied Thady to the limousine, Anne surreptitiously slid her hand over her stomach. Her period had been due yesterday. Of course, it might simply be delayed because of all the hectic activity leading up to opening night, but it gave her a wonderful glow of inner happiness to think it might be due to another cause. It was possible that Thady might consider marriage if she bore him a child.

She wouldn't ask him to.

But he might.

The premiere of *The Long Cold Winter* was a triumphant night for everyone. From the opening scene to the final curtain, the audience was enthralled. Tom Colby was utterly riveting in the main role. Passion simmered through the rest of the cast. The sets Anne had designed captured each shift of mood, subtly adding more power to the climax, which, when it came, was totally electrifying.

Yet over and above anyone else's contribution, the night belonged to Thady Riordan. His genius for dramatic theatre was on spell-binding display. When the final curtain came down, the audience was still caught up in the heart-twisting emotion of the last act. The awed silence was only broken by muffled sobs, sniffs, the surreptitious blowing of noses, the rustle of handkerchiefs being hastily drawn or put away.

The applause broke slowly, gathered momentum, growing to an ovation. No matter what their usual mode of behaviour—sedate, complacent, sober, sophisticated, cynical—the whole audience rose in acclaim.

The curtain calls went on and on, but the wild response from everyone in the theatre was not really for the cast. It had been drawn from them by the creator of all they had just seen and heard and felt.

For Anne, this new insight brought the sobering realisation that Alex Korbett had spoken no more than the absolute truth. Thady Riordan was the genius of his generation, perhaps the greatest playwright of the twentieth century. If he had to be alone to write, she had no right to stop him.

There was pandemonium in the foyer afterwards. Anne caught a glimpse of Alex in the crowd. He blew her a kiss and flashed a thumbs-up sign. She was glad that their old friendship had not been harmed by her promise to Thady.

Profuse congratulations were showered on both of them as Thady steered Anne through the excited melee to the street. He could have basked in adulation if he had wanted to, but he brushed it all aside, wanting only to be alone with her. Their limousine was waiting. They were off and away before they could be caught by the people spilling out of the theatre after them.

They held each other for a long time that night, aware that the production they had shared was now behind them. The exhilaration of its success meant little compared to the sense of time running out on this phase of their lives.

The few days left to them were punctured by endless telephone calls, requests for interviews, flowers and telegrams of congratulations arriving, constant interruptions. It seemed they were hardly ever alone except at night. The time of separation grew inexorably closer, yet the thought uppermost in their minds was never spoken. They couldn't talk about it. It was in their eyes, in every touch, in the way they made love.

Thady accompanied Anne to Heathrow to see her off on her flight to Australia. The parting was too painful to prolong. There were no words to say, no promises asked or given. One fierce kiss goodbye and Anne walked away from the man she loved.

But she carried one promise for the future with her. Anne was sure she was pregnant.

CHAPTER FOURTEEN

ANNE'S WELCOME HOME was somewhat strained. To Leonie Tolliver, not even fame and success at an international level made Anne's relationship with Thady Riordan any more acceptable. He was taking advantage of Anne. The fact that he had chosen not to accompany her home condemned him as a man who was wasting Anne's time. It proved, beyond doubt, that he had no serious intentions.

Anne side-stepped the issue as much as she could, busying herself with visits to her two married sisters, Liz and Kate, minding their children while they did Christmas shopping. Yet both Liz and Kate showed a quiet concern about where their oldest sister was heading in her private life. Jenny was also disappointed that her hopes and plans for Anne had been somewhat dashed by Thady's absenting himself from her sister's side. Luckily preparations for the wedding provided some happy distraction.

The wedding was lovely. The dresses Anne had designed were pure fairytale romanticism, and all the guests remarked how absolutely right they were for Jenny and her bridesmaids. Brian looked transfixed by the sight of his bride coming down the aisle, and after the marriage ceremony, both he and Jenny radiated blissful happiness.

Anne had to blink away a rush of emotional tears. She told herself that weddings were simply superficial, sentimental shows of love, meaning little in the long run of any relationship. Nevertheless, she could not quite quell the ache of yearning for the kind of public commitment Jenny and Brian had made to each other.

It was harder to hold back the tears when Jenny gave her a farewell hug before going off on her honeymoon. "Thanks so much for everything, Anne. Without you, my wedding wouldn't have been nearly as beautiful as it was."

"Nonsense! You and Brian made it beautiful."

Jenny hesitated a moment, searching Anne's eyes. "You are happy with Thady, aren't you? You're sure it's right for you?"

"Very happy," Anne assured her. "No other man could be more right for me."

Jenny's smile was tinged with relief. "That's all right, then. He's sure to come round to marriage in the end. Don't take any notice of Mum's rantings."

Anne tried to use Jenny's unflagging optimism to bolster her confidence in Thady's love for her. Her pregnancy had been confirmed. She was going to have Thady's child, but she had no idea how Thady was going to react to the news that he was going to be a father.

She wanted him to be thrilled, as Brian would most certainly be if Jenny had such news for him. Nevertheless, Anne had no idea what Thady's response might be. If he was disapproving or censorious, the happiness they had shared together might never be recaptured. Anne did her best to dismiss such disquieting thoughts.

Nevertheless, the festive period of Christmas and New Year was a lonely time for her. Liz, Kate and Jenny had their husbands beside them, and Thady was an ocean away. Despite the kinship of family, Anne had to continually fight the sense of not belonging anymore.

Somehow she had grown past them, or their realities were no longer hers. She yearned to be back in the flat in London, waiting for Thady's return. Even if he wasn't there, she could at least feel his presence in the home they shared.

This need drove Anne to change her flight to an earlier one. She told herself she wanted the flat to be warm and welcoming for Thady's return mid-month, so she arrived in England on the eighth of January.

Thady did not come home on the fifteenth. In the following days, Anne was caught up in a churning circle of anticipation and disappointment. Any minute now, she kept thinking, but the minutes passed with taunting slowness, and still Thady did not come home. Days crept into weeks. The month of January came to an end.

The weather was bleak—wet, grey and freezing cold, adding its miserable weight to the growing bleakness in Anne's heart. There was no message from Thady to revive anticipation of their soon being together. The silence from him stretched on and on, wearing out all Anne's excuses for it.

It seemed uncharacteristic of Thady not to consider her feelings. Even if he was involved with his writing, he could have spared her a thought, couldn't he? One phone call to appease her concern?

Anne began to worry that something had happened to him. Perhaps he was in a hospital somewhere, unable to contact her for some reason. She dismissed the chilling thought that he could have died. The death of Thady Riordan would not go unreported by the media. Yet if he was alive, it seemed that she was dead to him.

As difficult as that was to accept, Anne was slowly becoming resigned to it by mid-February. She received a call from Thady's agent, who had agreed to represent her business interests, as well. Was she interested in doing the production design for an updated version of *The Pirates of Penzance?*

Anne had no idea what Thady was doing, or when she might be required to work on his next play. Common sense urged that it was better for her to get on with her life and keep busy. She had a child's future to consider. Thady might never write again, might never appear in her life again.

She called Paula Wentworth, ostensibly to check if she was legally free to accept career commitments besides those she had signed for with Thady. What she really wanted to find out was whether Paula knew anything about Thady's present situation.

"You're free to take on any work you wish, any time at all," Paula assured her.

Anne swallowed the humiliation of her own ignorance to ask, "How long do you think it will be before Thady will have more work for me, Paula?"

"I can't tell you, Anne. I simply don't know."

"Then do you know when he'll be back in London?" Anne pressed.

There was a nerve-tearing silence. Then in a soft sympathetic voice, Paula asked, "You haven't heard from him, Anne?"

"No. Not a word. Has he been in touch with you?"

Another long, agonising pause. "I hope you understand that I'm bound by confidentiality to a client, Anne," Paula said slowly.

"Can you tell me if he means to come back to London?" Anne asked in desperation.

"That's up to Thady," came the cautious reply.

"Paula, is Thady all right?" Anne pleaded, casting all pride aside in her need to know *something*.

A deep sigh. "Anne, I don't know what to say to you. I spoke to Thady yesterday. He's still in America. He sounded tired . . . exhausted . . . torn apart."

The anguish in Paula's voice sent a shiver of apprehension down Anne's spine. "Please tell me what's wrong, Paula. You're keeping something from me, you and Thady. And I think Alex must know, as well. Don't you see I've got to know? I can't go on like this."

"Anne, I've said too much already."

Anne could feel her clamming up, retreating from further disclosure. With a sense of sinking hopelessness, she said, "Then tell me what to do, Paula. You know more than I do. Give me your best advice."

"If you want my professional advice..."

"Yes, I do."

"Be independent. Lead your own life. Fulfil the wonderful talent you have. Forge a future for yourself."

"That's all?" Anne asked, pleading for some ray of hope to cling to. The advice Paula had given was totally damning of any future with Thady.

"No. That's not all," Paula answered, as though dragging the words out against her better judgement. There was a long, ragged sigh. Then in a voice that shook with emotion, "As a woman, and as a friend to you, if you love Thady Riordan, if you truly love him, Anne, be there for him when he does come back. Don't ask questions. Accept him as he is. There's no other way."

The line was instantly disconnected. Paula Wentworth had said all she was going to say, and her deep caring for Thady left an indelible impression on Anne. One message was clear. Whatever torment Thady was going through, Anne was to be kept separate from it.

Whether this was to protect her from pain, or to help Thady shut out his own pain when he was with her, Anne did not know and could not begin to guess. He had lived like a monk, a hermit, a man condemned to a world of loneliness until she had forced herself into his life, claiming a need for him.

Anne suddenly realised that Thady would never say he *needed* her. He would never put any claim on her. Whatever the reason, or impediment, he felt he had no right to tie her to him in any but a professional sense. He had neither expected nor hoped for the happiness he had known with her. But he wanted it. And needed it. That was the other message Paula had tried to put across.

Tired . . . exhausted . . . torn apart. Was it some dreadful illness that required regular treatments in America? Thady had insisted that whenever he went to America, he had to be by himself. So whatever was happening to him now was going to happen again. And again.

Her hand slid protectively over her stomach. What had she done in conceiving Thady's child? Would her pregnancy be a further torment for Thady? A torment for both of them? She had been completely and utterly selfish in wanting his baby, and wantonly reckless in not discussing it with him beforehand.

It was too late to worry about that now. In fact, worrying about what she didn't know was probably the most futile thing she could do. If she didn't make some positive decisions about her life, she would go mad in this waiting vacuum.

Best to keep her mind busy on something else, she told herself, and promptly rang her agent to say she *was* interested in the offered production design and would like to meet with the director of the show as soon as possible. Since she would be working in London, there was little likelihood of missing Thady when he came back. If she happened to be out of the flat, he would certainly know she was still living there, waiting for him.

Driven by the need for some absorbing activity, Anne went out and bought a compact disc of Gilbert and Sullivan's *The Pirates of Penzance.* She immersed herself in the words and music so she'd be totally familiar with both when she went to the meeting where the updated concept of the show was discussed. She threw herself into work, blocking out all other concerns as she evolved her designs for the production.

The days passed relatively quickly. It was only when she went to bed that Anne was haunted by thoughts of Thady. There was little she could do about those dark hours. The night was always lonely.

On the last day of February Alex Korbett called to offer his congratulations on Anne's snagging what he called a plum job. When he invited her out for a celebratory dinner with him, Anne was sorely tempted to go, despite her promise to Thady. It was an opportunity to open Alex up, pressing on their old friendship to get the information she wanted. Yet that would be a breach of trust. She pleaded a headache and declined the invitation.

She lay awake that night, thinking of all the questions she might have asked Alex. She wondered if it would have done her any good to know the answers. Thady did not think so. Neither did Paula. Perhaps Alex would have been of the same opinion.

Sleep finally put a halt to the miserable treadmill of her thoughts, but even that was made restless by haunting dreams of phantoms forever out of reach. It was a relief to struggle free of yet another frustrating dream and wake to the brightness of morning. Anne listlessly thought there was a different quality about the light, but it took a few moments to realise what it was.

Sunshine was beaming through the bay window, sparkling sunshine without the dulling grey filter of clouds. The miseries of the night were instantly dispelled. Sunshine was definitely a good omen, she thought whimsically. It even seemed to bring the smell of spring flowers to banish the sterile bleakness of winter.

She breathed in deeply, enjoying the scent in the air. Her heart gave a funny jerk as she realised she wasn't imagining it. The smell of spring flowers *was* in the air! She sat up very abruptly, her eyes wide awake. Resting on the pillows on Thady's side of the bed was a glorious array of spring flowers!

Her heart turned over.

There was no hesitation about what to do, how to react, what she should think. Anne whirled out of bed and flew through the flat, her whole body pumping with excitement and happiness. Thady had come home to her.

She found him sprawled full length on one of the black leather sofas. The sight of him brought Anne's flying feet to a faltering halt. He was asleep, but that was not what stopped her from rushing to throw her arms around him in loving welcome. It was the shock of seeing how dreadful he looked.

He had lost so much weight that his face seemed to have no flesh on it at all. The skin was stretched tight over his cheekbones and jaw. The hollows in his cheeks had drawn deep lines on either side of his mouth. The dark shadows around his eyes made them look bruised and sunken in their deep-set sockets, a stark contrast to the glistening paleness of his forehead. Anne's heart contracted in fear and horror at what Thady must have been through to bring him to this awful state.

She wanted to take him in her arms and comfort him as one would a wounded child, cushioning his head against the softness of her breasts and tenderly stroking his hair. But he looked so tired and drained it seemed wrong to wake him. Anne contented herself with the gentlest of touches, a feather-light caress of her fingertips that assured her of the live warmth beneath the pale skin of his face.

His eyes flicked open. "I thought I felt the touch of an angel," he murmured, in the soft Irish lilt that curled her toes.

"Thady...oh, Thady." Tears swam into her eyes.

It seemed that Thady's strength had not been weakened by his loss of weight, for the next instant Anne was hauled onto the sofa with him, and he was leaning over her, his lips warmly sweeping away the moistness of her tears. "I want you so badly. Say that it's all right," he whispered, and the husky need in his voice was enough to dispel any doubts about what he felt for her.

"I'll always want you," she answered with a heart so full it felt it would burst.

A tremor ran through his body. His mouth claimed hers with a passion that hungered for the response she had promised him, and she gave it without reservation, wanting to fill him with her own life force.

She felt Thady's body harden, tighten, pulse with the wild primitive need to take all she offered. There was no fatigue in the arms that lifted her and carried her to the bedroom, no falter in the legs that strode forward with purpose. The green eyes blazed with an inner fire that demanded all-consuming attention.

"The flowers!" Anne cried as they both tumbled onto the bed.

Thady swept them aside, totally careless of where and how they might land. "*You* are spring to me," he said, and he made love to her with the ardour of a desperate man.

The intensity of his desire for her was both exciting and disturbing to Anne. It completely obliterated any possible doubt that Thady wanted her, yet the wanting seemed to be driven by a need to absorb all the warm, vital pleasures of her body. His whole being was concentrated on now. With her. In her.

There was a hungry possessiveness in the way he held her to him when he rolled onto his side. The desire to feel her around him was far from diminished by one release of sexual tension. Urgency gave way to a deep, pervasive sensuality, and every movement was piercingly sweet.

Anne could not bring herself to question anything as long as he was with her. Simply to have him again was enough. The world could end and she wouldn't care as long as she was in his arms.

She moved her head on the pillow to look at him, wanting to see her own contentment on his face. His eyes were closed, but there was a soft smile of pleasure on his lips. She reached up and lightly traced it with her fingertips, rejoicing that he looked as though he felt life was worth living.

The thick black lashes lifted to show a glimmer of deep green. He lifted a hand to her face, gently stroked her cheek, then trailed his fingers through the long, silky tresses of her hair. There was tenderness in his touch, and his smile gathered a loving indulgence.

"I've got something to tell you," she said impulsively.

"Tell me," he softly invited.

She hesitated. She knew that she had to tell him he was going to become a father, but was this the right moment? Would she lose all they had just shared? Would he leave her again? A shiver of apprehension ran down her spine.

"I've taken on the production design for *The Pirates of Penzance*," she said weakly.

He gave her a quizzical look. "Is that good or bad for you?"

It was much simpler to pursue a side issue than to face the critical moment that might change her life.

"That depends on you, Thady," she said slowly. "I didn't know if you'd need me. If you'd been writing."

His smile dipped into a grimace. "I haven't done any writing. At least, none of any importance. I have no work for you, Anne," he stated flatly.

Whether he had some problem with inspiration, or whether he had tried and failed to put into words what he felt, Anne couldn't guess. It was all too obvious that he had been through several kinds of hell while he had been away from her, and she felt no inclination to remind him of it.

"Is *Pirates* the kind of challenge you'll enjoy?" he asked, projecting interest in her work.

"Yes," she said, but she couldn't put any enthusiasm into it. There were more important things on her mind.

"That wasn't what you were going to tell me, Anne," he said quietly.

"How do you know that?" she asked, her voice sharp with anxiety. Did her body feel different to him? Had he guessed?

His eyes caressed her with soft caring, inviting her trust. "I felt you tremble," he said, revealing his intense awareness of her every physical reaction.

Resolution battled with apprehension. The moment for truth, for trust, was now. It could not be put off any longer. Her decision had been right for her. She could only hope it was right for Thady, as well.

She dropped her hand to his chest, spreading her palm over his heart, needing to feel it beating with hers. Her legs instinctively tightened around him. Still she found the words difficult to speak. Her throat had gone dry. She swallowed.

She met the calm steadiness of his gaze, forcing herself to watch for his reaction. Her lips felt stiff as they moved to shape the fateful sentences that formed relentlessly in her mind. They came out in a taut, flat monotone, belying the seething emotion behind them.

"I'm three months pregnant, Thady. You're a father."

CHAPTER FIFTEEN

ANNE SAW THE STUNNED LOOK in Thady's eyes, felt an abrupt pause in his breathing. There was a moment of utter stillness. Then his encircling arms drew her to him, pressing her close to his chest, his chin resting against her forehead.

"Was it an accident, Anne?" he asked quietly, his voice dull, totally void of any judgement.

Fear jammed Anne's mind. Had Thady deliberately hidden his face from her so that she couldn't see his reaction? She remembered his explanation for leaving her all those years ago, that he couldn't belong in her dreams of getting married, having children, the happy ever after.

"No, it wasn't an accident," she replied, a strong sense of self-determination rising over the fear. In a firm voice that would allow her to keep her distance from him if he disapproved of what she'd done, Anne calmly stated, "It was deliberate, Thady. Quite deliberate."

His arms tightened around her. A wash of relief eased Anne's inner tension. Thady did not want to let her go. Light warm kisses touched her hair, her temples, giving more soothing balm to her anxious mind.

"You're so brave. So independent," Thady whispered huskily. "Recklessly brave and fearlessly independent. You go after life as though there's no tomorrow, and nothing and no-one to fear."

There was deep admiration—almost awe—in his voice. While it sent a tingle of pleasure through Anne's heart, what Thady said seemed terribly ironic.

"It isn't all that easy," she demurred dryly. Then, because she ached to hear him say it, she asked, "Do you want our baby, Thady?"

He didn't answer. He rocked her in his arms. She felt a warm drop of moisture run down her forehead. Alarm bells jangled in Anne's mind. Thady was crying.

Yet if he admired her decision, didn't that mean he wanted her to have the baby? Why should he have such a reaction unless there was something to fear?

In frantic urgency, Anne pulled herself away so she could look at him. As he reluctantly released her from his embrace, she disentangled herself from him to sit up and assert her need to know all that concerned her.

"What's the matter, Thady?" she cried, her eyes sharply focussed on gathering every flicker of expression on his face.

His thick lashes were spiky from the heavy wetness of tears. Thady ruefully dashed his fingers over his cheeks. He mustered a crooked half-smile.

"I don't think I've ever felt so happy before. So much at peace with the world." His voice was a deep throb of emotion that gathered even more poignancy as he added, "I never thought I'd ever have a child."

"Why, Thady? Why did you think that?" she asked, probing his eyes for the truth.

"I never thought that anyone would do this for me," he answered simply. Then he leaned over and kissed her stomach, his lips pressing soft, adoring homage to the life within. "I'll love our baby, Anne," he whispered.

Tears pricked at her eyes as an inner voice cried, *But what about me? Why can't you say you love me?*

Anne quickly stifled it. She *knew* that in some special unique way Thady did love her, and one day, she promised herself, she would *make* him say it, even if he never married her.

More important at this moment was the question that had been at the forefront of her mind every day for the past three months. Her fingers ran slowly through the curls of his hair, gently holding him to the child he had accepted.

"Thady..." she began hesitantly.

"Mmm?"

Anne scooped in a quick breath and poured out the critical words. "There's no reason why I shouldn't have your baby, is there?"

He kissed her stomach again. "None whatsoever, from my point of view."

"There are no hereditary factors that should be taken into account?" she persisted.

He lifted his head, his eyes still shining happily as he propped himself on his side and gave her an indulgent smile. "Anne, it's perfectly normal you should worry like this, but I promise you, to the best of my knowledge, there are no genetic problems from my family that could harm our baby.''

He circled the soft roundness between her hips with reverent fingertips. ''We are going to have the most perfect, most adorable, wonderful child that has ever been conceived,'' he declared. Then he grinned infectiously as he trailed his fingers up to her breasts and began to circle them. ''You will be a perfect mother. And I'll try to be a perfect dad.''

There was no doubt that he genuinely believed what he said. Anne's relief spilled into an answering grin. It was pure bliss to be assured the baby was not at risk. Not only that, Thady had just committed to being more than the biological father of their child. That must mean he saw a future of sharing their lives together.

At least, as long as he could.

A huge question mark about *his* health still remained. Anne was intensely conscious of it as he leaned over to kiss her. His collarbones had hollows above them, and despite the softening effect of his grin, his face was far too gaunt.

''I think I'll have to make love to you again,'' he murmured, brushing his lips seductively over hers.

''No,'' she said decisively.

''Why not?'' He shot her a quizzical look. ''Will it affect the baby?''

''No. But you're having no more sex from me until you put on ten kilos,'' she teased, then added more seriously, ''you've lost an awful lot of weight.''

He made a self-mocking grimace. "I don't feel good to you?"

"So good that I don't want you fading away on me." Her eyes searched his worriedly. "Is there something wrong, Thady?"

"I guess I need you to stir an appetite for life," he answered, dismissing her concern with casual ease. He cocked a teasing eyebrow. "Do you suppose there's enough food in the kitchen for me to put on ten kilos over breakfast?"

That was it, Anne thought with a sense of helplessness. She could almost feel the shutters going up on the past three months. But she would make the future her business, she vowed, as she swung her legs off the bed and reached for her robe.

"I'm going to cook you a whopping big breakfast, Thady Riordan, and you'd better eat every bit of it," she warned.

He did.

Within weeks Thady was looking far more like his former self, and there was no doubting his appetite for life. He exuded happiness and contentment. He fussed over Anne, insisting that she hire assistants to do all the legwork involved in getting the materials for her production design for *Pirates*. When she had to go somewhere, he accompanied her to make sure she didn't exert herself. Anne laughed over his obsessive care for her, but she was secretly glad he cared so much.

He bought books on prenatal care. He bought books on bringing up children. No father-to-be could have been more assiduous in preparing for the birth of his child.

Most of the time Anne was delighted by his attitude, yet she could not help wondering about the reasons that inspired it. Did Thady know that his future was curtailed? Was that why he was so intent on having all he could while he could? He seemed to be centring his entire world around her and the baby. He did not attempt to write. He only went into his study to check the fax machine for messages.

One thing made no sense at all to Anne. If Thady had always wanted a child, the simplest way to go about it was to marry. If he had married her seven years ago, they could have had a family by now.

But then perhaps he wouldn't have written his plays. It seemed one way of life excluded the other for him. He had to be alone to write. That was what he had told her. Maybe he had forced himself to be alone in America for those three months, but it didn't work for him anymore because she had become more important to him.

He was still not prepared to offer marriage, not even for the baby's sake. That became painfully clear when Thady handed her a copy of a long legal document setting out all the details of a trust fund to give both her and their child financial security for life.

"Thady, we haven't even had the baby yet," she protested, stunned by the generosity of the settlement.

"I want to make sure you'll both be taken care of, no matter what happens," he answered.

"Are you expecting something to happen?" she asked sharply.

He shrugged. "Who can foretell the future? If I'm run over by a bus tomorrow, I don't want you having to work to support our child, Anne. The trust fund will pay for a nanny if you want to work, but if you'd prefer to be a full-time mother, then you'll have that option open."

"Wouldn't it be simpler..." She bit down on her tongue, cutting off the treacherous words. She had promised not to try to change him.

He raised his eyebrows questioningly.

She dropped her gaze to the legal document and shrugged. "I guess you've covered all contingencies."

He nodded. "Paula is very thorough. If you ever have a problem, Anne, go to her and she'll sort it out for you."

Paula, who knew everything, Anne thought, but she forced a smile over her niggling frustration. "You didn't have to do this, Thady. It was my decision to have a baby."

"Our baby," he reminded her. "And not all the money in the world could ever repay you for such a gift to me, Anne."

She didn't want money. She wanted him. But when he wrapped her in his arms and kissed her with intense passion, Anne told herself she had to do the same as Thady and live each moment together to the fullest.

Unfortunately that concept had no appeal for Anne's mother. Leonie Tolliver had no appreciation for a man who did not offer marriage to a woman he'd made pregnant. Especially when that woman was her daughter. Ever since Anne had written to announce the baby's arrival sometime in August, her mother's letters were peppered with pointed comments.

One of these remarks, however, did give Anne pleasure. "Jenny has just learnt she is pregnant. Of course, I don't have to worry about my youngest daughter since she has a husband to take care of her. Brian might not be rich or famous, but he's a decent hardworking man whom I can trust to do the right thing by Jenny."

Anne's correspondence with Jenny was in a much happier vein. Her youngest sister was a source of loyal support for everything Anne did.

The Pirates of Penzance opened in June. The theatre critics gave fulsome praise to the innovative production design by Annelise Tolliver. The gossip columnists made comment that Annelise Tolliver looked noticeably pregnant at the premiere. She was, of course, escorted by her constant companion, the playwright Thady Riordan, who seemed to have eschewed writing in favour of approaching fatherhood.

The next month was taken up with looking at houses. Thady had decided that a city apartment was not the best environment for bringing up a child. He was determined on a place in the country, not too far from London so that Anne could easily commute if she wanted to. When they finally found a house they both liked, Thady insisted on buying it in Anne's name.

He had Paula Wentworth draw up the necessary documents. Paula was as discreet as always, carrying out Thady's instructions without so much as a questioning comment. In fact, when Anne went to her office to complete the legalities, Paula wore an approving smile throughout the whole process.

Anne felt dreadfully uncomfortable about accepting a house as well as an income, yet she knew that it was all part and parcel of Thady's determination to protect both her and their child. She had come to believe Jenny was right in her reading of Thady's motives. Right or wrong, he had been protecting her all along. The only problem was that Anne still didn't know what he was protecting her from.

She looked at Paula as she finished the last signature and ruefully remarked, "This makes me feel like a kept woman."

Paula laughed. "I don't think kept women get to keep as much as this, Anne. You're actually better off, in security terms, than most married women."

Before she could stop herself, Anne blurted out the burning question. "Why doesn't Thady marry me, Paula?"

A mask of caution instantly fell over the other woman's amusement. There was a momentary flash of sympathy in the grey-green eyes, but even that was quickly muted to a calm, impassive look. "Aren't you happy the way you are, Anne?" she asked quietly.

"It's not that I'm unhappy...."

"Then leave well enough alone," Paula advised. "You know I can't discuss any of Thady's private business with you."

"Yes, I know. I'm sorry, Paula. It's just that—" she offered an appeasing smile "—I'm getting a lot of flack from my mother."

It was a weak excuse for treading once more on Paula's ethics, but it was graciously accepted. "It's an easy trap for parents to fall into, trying to lead their children's lives for them." The sympathetic comment gathered more point as Paula softly added, "Or the lives of those we care about. Unfortunately, more often than not it drives them away from us."

The subtle warning was not wasted on Anne.

Accept or lose.

It was, more or less, the same message Paula had spelled out months ago.

Since the last thing Anne wanted was to lose Thady, she would go on accepting whatever he chose to give her, do for her, share with her.

It was a happy, exciting time leading up to the birth of their baby. They shopped for nursery things. They changed their minds a thousand times over what names they favoured for their child. Thady bought books and magazines on home decoration and gardening. They spent hours planning the furnishings for their new home in the country and working out how to make best use of the grounds surrounding it.

Then, barely two weeks before the baby was due, Anne's world with Thady suddenly started falling apart. There was no cataclysmic bolt of lightning to mark the moment. Anne had no sense of unease, no premonition at all as she went to the kitchen to cook the big breakfast she insisted Thady have every morning. As usual, he went to the study to check his fax machine before joining her in the kitchen.

The eggs and bacon were cooked, toast made, everything ready to serve, except Thady wasn't there to serve it to. Anne called for him to come. There was no answer. She set the breakfast on the table and hurried through the flat to the study, thinking that he'd been distracted by something and hadn't heard her call.

The door was open.

He stood by the fax machine, a sheet of paper in his hands, his gaze fixed on whatever was printed on the page. His face had lost all colour. His mouth was set in a grim line. His body was utterly still.

"Thady?" Anne called sharply, feeling an urgent need to claim his attention, to pull him back from wherever he'd gone.

His head lifted with agonising slowness and turned towards her. There was a dull, faraway look in his eyes. His gaze dropped to her bulging abdomen, and she saw pain cross his face.

"What is it?" she cried, a nameless fear clutching at her heart.

"Nothing." His mouth twisted into a savage grimace as his hands screwed up the fax transmission, compressed the sheet of paper into a tight ball, then dropped it into the wastepaper bin.

Anne did not know what to do in the face of that deliberate lie. "I called you for breakfast," she said weakly.

"I'm sorry. I didn't hear you." He forced a travesty of a smile as he walked over to her. "Let's go and eat then."

But he had no appetite. He picked at the food, swallowing a few bits of egg as though they choked him, pushing the rest around his plate, not even touching the bacon. He chomped on a piece of toast as though willing his teeth into mechanical movement. He washed the crumbs down with sips from his cup of tea.

Finally he gave up any pretence of being able to eat. "I've decided to go out for a while this morning," he stated flatly. His eyes made brief contact with hers. "Don't get up," he said as he pushed away from the table and rose to his feet. He flashed her another false smile. "I know how you enjoy sitting over your coffee."

He made no move to kiss her, as he normally did before leaving her anywhere. He strode out of the kitchen with obvious haste. Anne made no move to follow him. She felt completely paralysed, as though anything she did or said might tip some critical balance that had to be maintained if disaster was to be avoided. She heard the front door bang shut and felt the separation like a cut to the heart.

She sat over her coffee for a long time, trying to pretend that nothing important had happened. Thady would come back, and they would go on as before.

Except she couldn't convince herself of that. Something in that fax had taken him away from her. The sense of sharing, the togetherness, was gone.

The image of the screwed up ball of paper plagued Anne's mind. How could she fight what she didn't know? If she was losing Thady anyway, acceptance was not going to do her any good. She had to know what she was up against.

Her whole body seemed to ache in protest as she levered herself out of the kitchen chair. For the first time throughout her pregnancy Anne felt ugly and cumbersome. She remembered the pain on his face when he had looked at her child-heavy body. Whatever else was claiming his mind and heart, he was torn by the want for the child he had never thought he would have.

Thady had shut the door to the study. Anne opened it. The time for shut doors in their relationship had been swept away this morning. She walked across the room and slowly dropped to her knees beside the wastepaper bin. Her hand shook as she reached for the fateful ball of paper. Her fingers trembled as they worked to smooth out all the twists and crinkles.

Anne felt no sense of guilt for wanting to read what had been written. There was no longer any trust to be kept for the sake of staying together in harmony. This was simply the long-delayed moment of truth that had to be faced.

CHAPTER SIXTEEN

THE MESSAGE was short and succinct.

> The decision has been made.
> The date is August twenty-first.
> If there's anything either Richard or I can do, you
> have only to ask. Our deepest sympathies go out
> to you at this time.
>
> Paula

Anne's mind whirled in confusion. She hadn't considered a legal problem. Surely that was what it had to
be, since Paula was involved. Yet what legal problem
would draw such a reaction from Thady?

Anne studied the words over and over again, trying
to find more significance in them, but there was nothing of any real substance to work on. The decision and
the date had evoked Paula's deepest sympathies, so
whatever was happening was final, and Paula saw no
way out of it.

Anne did not doubt the finality. It was what she had
seen and felt coming from Thady this morning. However, what lay behind it still remained a mystery. Anne
screwed up the paper and dropped it in the bin. She
would have to wait for answers.

The morning dragged by. It was midafternoon when Thady returned to the flat. Anne was lying down on one of the black leather sofas in the lounge. She felt sick from the ferment of uncertainties that had been stirred by Paula's message. When she heard the front door open, she instantly swung herself into a sitting position, determined to confront the situation head-on.

Whatever Thady had been doing while Anne had suffered through the wretched hours of worrying, he didn't look any the better for it. He entered the room without any awareness that Anne was there. His shoulders were slumped. His face was pale and strained from some inner torment, yet there was grim resolution etched on it.

"You've been a long time," Anne remarked as lightly as she could.

His head jerked towards her. His feet came to a halt. He stared at her as though from a great distance, as though she was a stranger who meant nothing to him. Anne's stomach churned, making her feel nauseous. It hurt to see the effort it took Thady to collect himself.

"I had a lot to do," he said quietly.

"Why don't you tell me what's wrong, Thady?" Anne accused more than asked. It was impossible to ignore what was so painfully clear.

He grimaced at her bluntness. The green eyes looked as sick as she felt as he walked down to the lounge area. He did not come directly to her. He did not sit down with her. He picked up one of the ab-

stract sculptures from a side table and stood looking
at it, his fingers idly caressing its marble curves.

"I have to go to America, Anne. I have to go."
There was a driven note in his voice that denied any
argument.

Rebellion stirred in Anne. Three months of America had drained Thady of any appetite for life. The
effect of this morning's message on him had convinced her that nothing good was going to happen
there. Another visit would be damaging not only to his
wellbeing, but to their relationship, as well.

"When do you have to go?" she asked, trying to
keep calm and clear-headed.

"Tomorrow."

"For how long, Thady?"

He slowly replaced the sculpture on the table. He
met her gaze square on. "I don't know how long. It
may be weeks. It may be months. I simply don't
know."

Anne took a deep breath. "Then I'll come with you.
Our baby can be born there as well as here," she reasoned, determined not to be separated from him no
matter what the problem was.

He shook his head. "I've made arrangements for
you, Anne. You may not be able to manage here alone
when the baby starts coming. I thought it best if you
stay with Paula and Richard. They're happy to look
after you and make sure—"

"Will you stop thinking of what's best for me!"
Anne burst out with fierce indignation. She struggled
to her feet, ignoring the pain that shot across her lower

back. "*I* know what's best for me, Thady," she insisted. "I will be much happier going to America with you. In fact, I will be extremely unhappy if you leave me behind."

His face could have been carved from stone for all the effect her words had on it. "I can't have you with me, Anne."

"But you want to be with me for the birth of our baby," Anne cried in sharp protest. "How can you leave me now, after all we've done together, and when it's almost time for our child to be born?"

He turned abruptly away from her and walked over to the bay window. She saw his shoulders heave as he dragged in a deep breath. His head bowed, as though under an unbearable burden as he spoke.

"I'm sorry. I know I led you to expect I'd be with you at the birth of our child. But I can't be, Anne."

He was not only turning his back on her, but on their baby as well. His apology was no excuse to Anne. His absence at this time was unforgivable. She seethed with so many turbulent emotions, it was almost impossible to find some saving grace for the situation he was imposing on her. Her voice shook with the intensity of her feelings as she demanded an acceptable explanation.

"Give me one good reason, just one good reason. Why can't you be with me, Thady?"

He didn't answer.

"Thady, for God's sake! We're a family now. There shouldn't be any more of these unexplained separations. We may not be married, but wherever you go, we should be together."

"Anne, I've made what provision I could for my absence," he dragged out.

"That's not good enough, Thady."

"I told you it had to be this way a long time ago," he said wearily.

In a fury of hurt and frustration Anne hurled a bitter challenge at him. "Thady, if you won't give me a damned good reason I can't come with you, then don't bother coming back to me. I won't be here. And neither will your child."

His neck arched. He swung around to face her. "You'd do that to me? After all I've done for you?"

A rush of shame burned her cheeks, yet her mind still insisted that he wasn't being fair to their relationship. "You're deserting me when I most need you, Thady."

His face worked with emotion. "For your sake, I denied my own needs for seven years. Can't you wait a few months for me?"

"Why? Just tell me why!" she cried, unable to accept anything on blind faith anymore.

"For God's sake, Anne! Leave it alone!"

"No," she bit out vehemently. "I won't leave it alone. I don't want to be left alone again. Not for seven years, or seven months, or seven weeks, or seven days! Not without knowing why, Thady. I will not accept that anymore."

He exploded into agitated movement, pacing the floor. He threw her a tortured look. "I've tried to do the right thing by you. You wanted me, Anne. You said you needed me. You chose to have our child. I didn't ask it of you."

"You wanted me, too, Thady," she argued with feverish passion. "And you wanted the child."

"Yes. To my eternal damnation!" he rasped.

"Why do you say that?"

"Isn't it obvious?"

"No. Nothing is obvious."

"Well, it should be. It damned well should be," he muttered, angry frustration raging from him as he stormed around the room. "Why do you think I left you eight years ago?"

"I never understood that."

"I wanted you so badly. You brought me to life again, showed me joy, shared it, made me feel things that I'd thought were as good as dead. I knew it was wrong to give in to the attraction, but you were such a delight to me I couldn't resist it. Just for a while, I thought. Then you started getting serious, making plans, wanting promises I couldn't give. *Couldn't*, Anne. Doesn't that tell you something?"

She shook her head, unable to see that he was telling her anything different to what he had told her before.

"You don't want to see, do you?" he accused bitterly. "It's easier if I take the hard decisions. You still want to dream. It's up to me to face the realities that have to be faced."

"What realities are you talking about, Thady?"

"You said a career had taken the place of all your other dreams, but that wasn't true. You turned what I offered you into something else, Anne, tying me to a future that I couldn't guarantee."

His chest heaved with the turbulence of his feelings. His hands cut the air in vehement gesture as he threw more accusations at her. "Being with me, working with me...that was what you asked. But it wasn't enough for you, was it? So you decided to have a child. My child. Whom you're now using to blackmail me into staying with you when I can't."

Anne flinched. "It's not blackmail. You said you'd love our child. What kind of love is it that doesn't want to welcome a child into the world?"

"The kind of love that makes damned sure the child will never want for anything, no matter how impractical and starry-eyed its mother is!" Thady hurled at her. "We're not married, Anne. Nor are we as good as married. I never promised you marriage, nor did I leave you in any doubt about my position on that score. Why else do you think I set up a trust fund and bought you a house?"

"I haven't asked you to marry me." She fought back. "Only for us to be together. And you still haven't told me why we can't be."

"You don't want to know. If you'd wanted to know you would have worked it out by now."

"Well, I'm sorry I'm so dense!" She flung the words at him. Then, in sheer desperation, she begged, "Tell me, so I can make sense out of it, Thady."

He stopped pacing. The pain on his face, the haunted look in his eyes were terrible to see. "I've tried to protect you from this," he said harshly.

For a moment Anne wavered in her resolution. But she had to know. It had all gone too far for her not to know now.

"I'm married, Anne. I was married long before I met you. And for all that my wife and I haven't lived together for over ten years, she is still my wife. And we are still married."

If it had been a flat statement, Anne might have withstood the shock better. But the words poured from Thady with a passion that smashed any possibility that the marriage was dead for him. All the dark passions in his soul, kept hidden from her... they revolved around this marriage that was far from dead.

Her head spun as she tried to fit the pieces of what she knew together. Thady leaving her to pursue her dreams, living like a monk except when driven to ease his physical frustrations, coming back to her when he thought she might accept him on equal terms, insisting she was free... as he had to be free to go back to his wife.

Anne swallowed hard, trying to regain some equilibrium. "You should have told me. From the beginning," she choked out.

He closed his eyes, shutting out the pain between them. "I didn't *want* to remember."

"Why not tell me the second time around?" she cried.

His eyes slowly opened, revealing a bleak weariness. His mouth twisted with irony. "It wasn't relevant initially. Then, when you revealed the damage I'd done, and your need for me...would it have been better or worse for you if I'd told you I was married, Anne?"

She remembered the desperation of that night, her fear that Thady would reject her, her joy when he had received her into his embrace. If he had told her he was married...

"You said I was the only man for you," Thady reminded her harshly. "Would you have chosen adultery, Anne? Wasn't it better for me to bear that guilt and give you all I could of what you wanted? To let you be free of any moral torment so you could have what you needed from me?"

Anne shook her head, not knowing how she would have reacted. If she had known he belonged to another woman... "Your wife," she choked out. "Why hasn't she been living with you all these years?"

It was as though her question drained him of life. His face took on a frightening death-mask as he answered her. "She does live with me. In my heart. She always has and always will. The one great passion of my life."

Anne could feel the blood draining from her own face. "You love her...that much."

"Yes."

Not for Anne his love. That had been given to the woman he had married, irrevocably and forever, despite the fact that it wasn't returned, couldn't be returned, or there would be no separation. It was so unfair, so futile, just as her love for Thady was unfair and futile. He cared about her. He desired her. But he did not love her.

"You go to her in America," Anne said dully.

"Yes."

"But she doesn't want you to stay with her."

His face twisted. "God knows what she wants! I've done everything I can think of to reach her, to bring her back to me, but I can't break the barrier between us. I've beaten my head against it for months on end. Until my own survival and sanity depended on getting away from it. Mostly I've escaped into writing."

"Until I provided a happier escape," Anne said with bitter understanding.

"You've given me a lot of happiness, Anne," he acknowledged, his eyes boring into hers as he added, "I thought I'd given you some happiness, as well."

"Yes, you have," she acknowledged in return. *With no happy ending.* She couldn't accuse Thady of deceiving her about that. He had told her straight out he didn't belong in her dream of a happy ever after. She simply hadn't wanted to believe it.

"You forced this issue, Anne," Thady reminded her in a bleak tone. "The decisions are all yours now."

Her chin lifted in proud determination. Her amber eyes glittered with a fierce resolution to rise above the pain that seemed to be racking her body. Her hands moved to hug her unborn child to herself.

"I want to know why it's so imperative for you to go to your wife now. Why can't it wait for another couple of weeks?"

His gaze dropped to her protective hold of their baby. "I have to go," he bit out, his jaw tight as he once more turned away from her and walked to the bay window. His hands were clenched at his sides as he added, "My wife comes first. The child will be born whether I'm here or not. This is the last chance I have to bring my wife back to me."

"And if you can do that, you'll stay with her?"

"Yes. I'll stay with her."

"And if you can't, you'll come back to me. And our child. Is that the plan?"

She saw his hands unclench and clench again. "Do you want me to, Anne?"

No, she thought. She couldn't bear being second best. She couldn't live with him, knowing what she now knew. Anne had felt stabs of jealousy before, when she had seen photographs of Thady with other women, but the wave of jealousy that consumed her now was so intense she could not bear to stay in the same room with him.

Almost blind with the pain of it, she lurched her way past the furniture, down the hallway, into the bedroom where she had committed adultery countless times with a man who loved his wife. The wife who came first.

She staggered to the dressing table, opened the drawer where she kept the diamond earrings. She could not remember him kindly. Not after this. And he was never going to tell her he loved her, never going to marry her. She took out the velvet box. A pain sliced through her lower back. Liquid gushed down her legs.

Anne cried out in appalled horror as she thought she had lost all control. Then another pain hit her and she realised what had happened, realised that the pain had nothing to do with her heartbreak.

"Anne." Thady's voice called out in anxious alarm. "Anne." Running down the hallway.

Somehow she managed to turn to face him as he reached the bedroom doorway. She threw the velvet box at his feet. "Take them back! Give them to the woman you love!" she cried, then bent over, sobbing for breath as another contraction began.

"Anne, for God's sake . . ."

"If it's not . . . too much trouble, get me to the hospital . . . before you go."

CHAPTER SEVENTEEN

THADY WOULD NOT LEAVE HER when they got to the hospital. He remained at her side while she was being settled in a labour ward. Even after that he made no move to go.

"You don't have to stay," Anne told him, her eyes firing a fierce rejection of any further concern for her. "As you said, the baby will be born whether you're here or not. That's my responsibility. Mine alone, since having the baby was my choice."

His eyes begged her forbearance. "I want to stay, Anne."

Bitterness welled over her pain. Of course, he could stay now. His flight to America was booked for tomorrow. If her labour didn't go on for too long, he would get to see his child. The child he had never expected to have because his wife couldn't or wouldn't give him one.

"Please yourself," she said dully. "But don't expect any joy from it."

"Anne..." He took her hand, his fingers working over hers in intense agitation of spirit. "Anne, you won't transfer your...your hatred of me onto the child, will you?"

"It's *my* child. Mine," she answered with vehement possessiveness. "I don't need you anymore, Thady. And *we* don't need your trust fund, either. Nor your house. Nor the career you gave me. As soon as I'm able, I'll take my baby home to Australia with me and start a new life. Without you in it!"

She snatched her hand out of his and rolled her cumbersome body over on the bed so she was facing away from him. After several long, silent moments she heard him settle on a chair to wait out the hours with her. Anne was determined not to look at him again. Let him see his child, she thought savagely. Let him see what he was giving up for the wife who didn't deserve his love.

Oddly enough, his presence eased the loneliness of the pain she suffered through, even though they didn't talk to each other. The only words spoken were to doctors and nurses.

The baby was born just after three o'clock the next morning.

Anne was so exhausted, she did not have the strength to protest when the nurse passed the newly wrapped baby to Thady for him to bring to her. She watched him cradle it tenderly, his face softened with love and wonderment as he slowly walked to Anne's side. Very gently he placed the precious bundle next to her, then bent to kiss the soft little face.

"I wish you every blessing in life, my son," he whispered huskily. He straightened up, his hand trailing over Anne's to draw her attention. "Thank you," he said simply.

He turned away before she could make any reply. He was gone before she realised there was nothing appropriate to say, anyway. It was over. Thady had accepted her decision.

As she looked down at the tiny perfection of her baby son, the emptiness Thady had left behind was filled by a flood of maternal love. She was glad it was a boy. A boy with tight black curls. Wanting Thady's love had been hopeless from the start, but she wouldn't be the loser with this part of him. His son was hers.

Eventually she was wheeled into a private room. She relinquished her baby into the care of the nursing staff and welcomed sleep long overdue.

It was almost noon when she awoke. Thady would have left London by now, she thought, and idly wondered what *was* scheduled for the twenty-first of August. Not that it was any of her business anymore. Even if it was a divorce action, it made no difference to her future. Today was the start of a new life with her son.

Michael John, she decided. Michael John Tolliver. It was a fine name. Thady had preferred Patrick for a son, but that no longer mattered. She would call her boy Michael John.

Her bedside table was cluttered with two beautiful floral arrangements. The accompanying cards had been left in easy reach for Anne. She picked them up, certain in her mind that neither of them would hold Thady's name. One was from Paula and Richard Wentworth, the other from Alex Korbett. Of course,

Thady would keep Paula informed, and Paula had probably told Alex about the birth since he was an old friend of Anne's.

A nurse made her entrance with yet another floral gift, white daisies and blue irises for a boy. "Ah, I don't have to wake you up," the nurse said cheerfully. "It's about time we fed you so you can feed your baby. My goodness, he's got a great pair of lungs when he starts bawling for his mum!"

Anne laughed with pleasure at the thought of her son wanting her, even if it was only to be fed.

"I'll put these down here, shall I?" the nurse asked, placing the new flowers on the movable tray at the end of Anne's bed. "They were ordered from Australia. How about that?" She gave Anne a big grin as she handed over the accompanying envelope.

Thady must have informed her family of the birth, Anne thought, quickly extracting the card from the envelope. Her eyes widened in surprise as she read the message.

"Thady called. He's arranged for me to fly to England to be with you and the baby. See you both in a day or two. Keep well. Love, Jenny."

Tears swam into Anne's eyes before she could stop them.

"Hey! Not bad news, I hope," the nurse crooned sympathetically.

"No. Good news," Anne assured her with a wobbly smile. "My sister is coming to visit."

"Lovely! Now I'll just bring you a nice cup of tea, and then order up your lunch."

Anne dwelled on this last kind and generous gesture of Thady's for a long time.

One couldn't order love. It was there or it wasn't there. Perhaps it was wrong of her to deny Thady access to their child. She had made that decision out of bitter personal pain, not with any thought to the future happiness of her child. Anne had no doubt that Thady would shower love on his son, if and when he could make time to be with him.

She decided she would have to give more thought to that. At a later date. When she felt more settled, when seeing Thady wouldn't hurt so much.

Tears filled her eyes again as she thought of Jenny dropping everything to fly to her side. Never mind her husband, Brian, who was probably concerned about his wife taking off for the other side of the world. Anne could just imagine Jenny laying down the law.

"Brian, Anne *needs* me. If you called Anne and said I needed her, she would come flying to me. That's what sisters are for."

And Brian would love Jenny all the more for it, Anne decided.

At least she had her baby to love. Michael John, she recited to herself, feeling her love for him swelling her heart with joy. She would never, never regret the decision she had made to have this child.

She thought it even more strongly when he was brought to her for feeding and she held him in her arms, watching his tiny hand curling and clutching at her breast, feeling the soft sucking motion that sent tingles right down to her stomach. Her life had been worth living simply for this wonderful experience.

Michael John was snugly nestled in the crook of Anne's arm when Paula Wentworth knocked on the door, breaking the private intimacy Anne was enjoying with her baby.

"Mind if I come in?" she asked, her smile appealing for entry.

Paula was so closely connected to Thady that Anne felt a twinge of reluctance about the visit, but she could not dismiss the friendship Paula had extended to her on any number of occasions.

"Please do. And thanks for the flowers, Paula."

"My pleasure. Is he asleep?" Paula whispered, her gaze dropping to the baby as she came forward.

"Yes."

"Oh, he's so beautiful!" Paula declared warmly. "The spitting image of Thady."

Anne's heart clenched at the comparison.

Paula reached out and pressed her hand. "I'm sorry Thady couldn't share this time with you, Anne," she said in soft sympathy.

"He had to go," Anne stated flatly.

"I know."

Anne took a deep breath as she told herself to use this opportunity to start separating herself from Thady's world. "Thady said he'd made arrangements for me to stay with you, but I won't, Paula. My sister's coming. I'll be fine with her."

"Of course. But if there's anything we can do, please don't hesitate to ask."

The concern in her voice drew a wry smile from Anne. "You don't have to be discreet anymore, Paula. Thady told me about his wife."

"Oh!" Paula looked momentarily disconcerted. She set a chair close to the bed and sat down. Her shrewd grey-green eyes registered understanding. "I guess that came as a great shock to you, Anne."

"Yes."

"The date..." Paula grimaced. "It was the worst possible timing for you."

"Yes," Anne agreed.

The grimace curved into an indulgent smile as Paula looked down at Michael John. "At least Thady was able to be with you for the birth. And to see his baby son. Such a lovely memory to take away with him."

Anne felt resentment stir. Paula had always been supportive of everything Thady did. Including adultery and deception.

Paula's gaze lifted in kindly inquiry. "Will your sister be staying in London until Thady comes back?"

"No. And neither will I. I'm not waiting for Thady this time, Paula. I'm going home to Australia. And staying there."

"You don't mean..." Paula frowned. "You can't mean you don't want him back?"

"He chose to leave me. For the wife he loves."

"But, Anne." Paula looked deeply distressed. She shook her head. "How can you be so cruel! It's only a matter of a few days and then it will all come to an end. A blessed release for both of them."

"It will never come to an end for Thady," Anne retorted sharply, angered by Paula's twisted view of who was being cruel to whom. "He loves her. He always will."

"Oh, Anne! You'd give up the reality of your love with Thady because of a remembered dream?"

It might be a memory but it was very real to Thady, Anne thought grimly. His one great passion. "His wife comes first with him," she stated bitterly.

"For God's sake, Anne! Can't you understand that at a time like this? Have you no compassion?" Paula demanded, her whole expression stamped with appalled horror.

"Why should I?"

Paula rose to her feet with frosty dignity. "I see Thady was right in wanting to keep you separate from that part of his life if this is your reaction to it. And after all Thady's done for you!" There was an icy contempt in her eyes. "You'll forgive me if I leave you to your incredible selfishness."

Paula made her exit while Anne was still swallowing the shock of that accusation. Paula's condemnation of her was so absolute it forced Anne to re-examine their conversation. The more she thought about it, the more she realised she had to be missing some important pieces of information about Thady and his wife.

As biased as Paula might be towards Thady's point of view, she was not an unreasonable person. Until now, she had been sympathetic towards Anne's position, but she had decisively insisted Thady's wife should come first at a time like this, and that Anne should have shown compassionate understanding.

The friendly nurse came in to take Michael John back to the nursery for a bath and change. Anne's mind was so busy revolving around these questions, she didn't mind giving in to hospital routine. She decided there was only one person who was likely to give her the answers she wanted. Alex Korbett. There was no reason to keep her promise to Thady anymore, and there could be very cogent reasons why she should break it.

She hitched herself up in bed and reached for the telephone on the table beside her. She breathed a sigh of relief when Alex promptly answered her call.

"It's Anne. Thank you for the lovely flowers, Alex."

"Only too delighted. Are you feeling very much the proud mother of your personal production design?"

Anne had to smile at his patter. "Very proud. But also rather lonely at the moment. Thady had to leave me to go to America. I need your company, Alex. Could you possibly..."

"Say no more. I was born to be a gallant knight to ladies in distress. I shall pop into a metal steed and gallop to your side. Now smile, dear girl, and count the minutes."

Barely half an hour later he arrived with an armful of glossy magazines. "They've got pretty pictures, if nothing else," he declared, settling on the chair Paula had vacated.

"Thanks, Alex. You're a treasure," Anne said warmly.

He preened in his extravagant manner. "Always full of goodies. But I don't open my treasure to everyone, you know. Only to special people." His bright blue eyes beamed their favour on her. "Where's the precious babe?"

"In the nursery ward. I'll show him to you later, Alex. Right now I need to talk to you about Thady and his wife."

His expression underwent an immediate change. His hands flapped in protest. "No, no, out of the question, dear girl. Can't be done. My lips are sealed on that subject. I don't want to be murdered. Thady said he'd kill me if I breathed a word. And he meant it. Very passionate about it. Can't be done."

"Alex, I know about his wife," Anne pointed out emphatically. "But I don't know enough. You've got to tell me what I don't know."

He shook his head vehemently and rose to his feet. "Sorry, Anne. Gave my solemn word. Can't help. Best if I go before I get into trouble."

"Alex, if you don't tell me, I'll leave Thady and take his son with me, and he won't be coming home to anyone because we'll be gone. Back home to Australia."

Alex sat down again, his mouth dropping open in shock. "You wouldn't do that to him, Anne."

"Yes, I would. I've already told Paula Wentworth that's what I'm going to do. And she said things to me that made me realise Thady hadn't told me everything about his wife. So if you think I should stay here for him, Alex, you'd better start telling me why."

Alex heaved a deep sigh. "Cleft stick," he muttered. "Damned if I do, and damned if I don't."

"You can start by telling me what's going to happen on the twenty-first of August," Anne bored on relentlessly.

"The machines," he said dolefully. "They're going to switch off the machines. Her family told Thady they were going to put an application to the court for that purpose when he went over there last December. Irreversible deterioration. No hope of a normal life anymore. Thady didn't feel he could fight them about it. The last ten years have been painful for them, as well. So the case went through the courts and they won the decision they wanted. And finally the date was set for the twenty-first of August."

Anne couldn't make much sense out of this information. "What machines, Alex?"

He frowned at her. "You said you knew about his wife."

"Just tell me what machines."

"I don't know. I'm not into that kind of medical technology. Whatever is involved."

"For what?"

"To keep her alive, of course. She's been in a deep coma for ten years. Can't do anything for herself. Isn't aware of anything or anyone. Just lies there in a deep coma."

"Oh, my God!" Anne clapped her hands to her face and stared at Alex in horror as all the pieces fell into place with devastating force.

"You didn't know," Alex said accusingly.

"Not about the coma," Anne choked out. "How did it happen? Was it an accident?"

"No." He shook his head. "That's the tragedy of it. They'd only been married for eighteen months. Still on their honeymoon, so to speak. Unknown to both of them she had Goodpasture's disease. One night when they were making love..."

"Go on," she urged.

Alex looked distinctly uncomfortable, but he acceded to her need to know. "She haemorrhaged severely into both lungs. Before Thady could get medical help for her, she'd virtually suffocated. She went into a coma and has never emerged from it."

He heaved a deep sigh. "Thady blamed himself for it. He found out all he could, everything that's ever been written about coma patients. Year after year he's gone and sat at her bedside, talking to her, writing his plays for her and reading them to her, doing all he can to bring her back."

And last Christmas he had been told about her family's decision to seek an end to the agony. Anne finally understood what Thady had been through while she had been waiting for him. He must have tried harder, longer, being with his wife day and night, torn apart by his inability to reach her.

It made sense now, his tears when she had told him about the baby. Having lived every minute with the imminence of a death sentence for the woman he loved, he had been granted a life to have in her place.

Alex leaned forward and took her hands. "Anne, my life is probably forfeit if Thady ever learns I've told you about this."

"How do you know it all, Alex?"

"Thady told me his circumstances when he asked me to give you a job eight years ago." He shrugged, then added, "Paula knows I know."

"I see," Anne murmured, then with puzzled curiosity asked, "how is it that there's been no publicity about any of this, Alex? What with the court case, and Thady being fairly famous..."

"His wife kept her maiden name when they married. And Thady didn't attend the court case. Besides, you must remember that Thady wasn't at all well known then. Apart from which, he keeps his visits to America very private. It would be crassly intrusive for the press to have a field day with such a painful situation."

Anne fully agreed on that. The press could be such vultures on what they euphemistically called human interest stories.

Alex squeezed her hands. His eyes filled with anxious appeal. "Anne, Thady doesn't want to lose you. He's had so little to be happy about over the years. You can't desert him now. Or rob him of his son. You must see that wouldn't be fair." His mouth made an eloquent grimace. "Besides which, he'll kill me. You mightn't think my life is important, but it is to me."

Anne managed a reassuring smile. "It's all right, Alex. You've been a good friend to both of us in telling me what you have."

He instantly brightened. "So you'll stay?"

"I don't know. I'll have to think about it. But there is one last thing you can do for me, Alex. Give me the address of the hospital."

"No." He waved his hands in truculent protest. "No. That's not a good idea, Anne."

"Give it to me, Alex," she commanded. "I don't know if I'll ever need it. Or use it. But if you don't give it to me, and things get fouled up between me and Thady, you'll be held responsible for it."

Alex turned green. "Why do I get involved in these things?" he cried despairingly.

"Because you want Thady Riordan to write more plays."

"Yes. Yes, I do. For that I would almost sacrifice my life."

"Then write down the address."

He heaved a very deep sigh, grimaced in resignation, then drew a slim notebook and a pen from the inner pocket of his suitcoat. "I hope this works out, Anne," he muttered as he wrote the address down.

"So do I," Anne agreed feelingly.

She didn't know what decision she would make. She had to look after her baby first. She had to wait until Jenny arrived from Australia. Only then would she be able to concentrate her heart and mind fully on what she was going to do about Thady.

CHAPTER EIGHTEEN

IT WAS wellnigh impossible for Anne to make a decision. To be with Thady at such a time seemed a ghoulish intrusion upon a deeply personal and private tragedy. Yet the alternative was equally unacceptable. Not to be with him at a time when he might need her strength and support to help him past such a traumatic event seemed dreadfully unfeeling.

In a way, this whole situation was his fault. He had kept his secrets right to the end, perhaps finding it unbearable to talk about what was to happen, particularly to the woman who had taken his wife's place in his life.

Guilt about infidelity, guilt about being happy with Anne while his wife's death was being decided in the courts, guilt about sharing the anticipation of having a baby instead of sticking to the task of reclaiming his wife from her coma. Anne could understand the emotional hell that had separated Thady from her when he had received that fateful fax. He would instinctively recoil from inviting Anne's pity or sympathy or compassion.

Clearly he did not want Anne with him while he strove to bring his wife back from the brink of death. He had to concentrate his entire life force on one last effort before it was too late. Anne knew he would spend every possible moment with his wife, barely sleeping, probably not eating, trying everything he knew to reach past the deep coma and touch her mind.

If the circumstances were reversed, and it was her husband under a death sentence, Anne knew she would do the same, despite the long passage of years that made their love more a remembered dream than a reality. She would not have been able to let him die without trying one last time.

But then the horror of the machines being switched off... And afterwards, the bereft emptiness, the grief for what had once been, the unchangeable finality, the cold loneliness of all the dark spaces. Thady had murmured those words to her on the night they had first made love, the night he had accepted her into his life. Anne couldn't bear the thought of Thady feeling that again, not when she could stop it by being there and assuring him he could come back to her and their baby when he was ready.

Yet how would that sound to him at such a moment? Maybe he would hate her for being alive when the wife he had loved was dead. Maybe he would see her arrival on the scene as some jealous attempt to claim him from his wife. Totally selfish.

Anne was still agonising over what she should do when Jenny arrived two days later. Despite the fatigue of the long flight from Sydney to London, Jenny did her best to be cheerful company, but Anne's emotional stress was so great she could barely respond to her sister. Nor was it doing her baby any good. Her milk dried up, and Michael John had to be bottle-fed.

Jenny grew anxious about Anne's withdrawn state. "I know you must be missing Thady, but, Anne," she pleaded, "you should be bursting with happiness about the baby, not sinking into some postnatal depression."

Somehow Jenny's plea triggered Anne's own tortured need for positive action. Right or wrong, she felt driven to go to the man she loved and show him the same kind of love and compassion he had shown her in answering her needs. She looked into the worried eyes of her youngest sister and appealed for understanding.

"Jenny, I've had to come to a decision that was very difficult to make. I need your help. I don't want to explain the whys and the wherefores."

"That's okay," Jenny encouraged. "I'll do anything you ask."

"I have to go to America to be with Thady. It's terribly important that I be there for him on the twenty-first of August. And that's only six days from now."

Jenny frowned in concern. "What about the baby?"

"Will you look after Michael John for me? I'll hire a nanny to help you. I can't take him with me. Very young babies suffer severe pain from the difference in air pressure in airplanes. One of the nurses explained it to me."

"Don't worry about it. He'll be fine with me," Jenny assured her. "I've had a lot of practice with Liz's and Kate's kids when they were babies."

"There are a couple of other matters, Jenny."

"Go on."

"An air ticket. On Concorde, if possible. I can't afford any delay."

"It's really that urgent?"

Anne projected all the inner certainty and intensity that she felt at Jenny. "This is the most important decision of my life. I'm full of fear. I have no idea what the outcome will be. It will determine what the future holds for Thady and me. And our son. Please don't make it worse by questioning."

Jenny leaned over and planted a loving kiss on her cheek. "Relax, Anne. Just tell me what you want and I'll get moving on it."

Over the next five days, Jenny was a source of indefatigable support. Somehow she managed to fulfil all Anne's requests, and never once gave into any curiosity about the situation. She was a tower of strength, particularly with caring for the baby. It tore Anne's heart to leave Michael John behind but she had no doubt about Jenny's competence to look after him.

Her inner tension virtually obliterated the lonely journey to her destination in America. Anne fiercely concentrated on blocking out any doubts about what she was doing. The decision was made. She was on her way. She would be at the hospital before the machines were switched off on Thady's wife.

If Thady had succeeded in bringing his wife out of the deep coma, then there would be nothing for Anne to do but turn around and go home. But if he had failed, she had to let him know he could share the dark, lonely spaces of his life with her again. If he wanted to.

Anne spent a restless night in her hotel room. She could not stomach the thought of breakfast the next morning. She dressed in the suit she had packed, a sage green outfit that she hoped was quietly appropriate and non-offensive should Thady see her at all. She wound her thick, long hair into a neat chignon, intensely conscious of not appearing in any way competitive for Thady's attention. Despite the paleness of fatigue and the shadows under her eyes, she eschewed make-up on the same delicate grounds.

A cab took her to the hospital. It was just nine o'clock as she walked through the entrance doors. One hour to go, she thought, her stomach churning with a thousand uncertainties. Anne wasn't sure where to go, whether she would even be able to gain admittance to the ward where Thady was undoubtedly with his wife, waiting through to the last fatal second. Her legs trembled as she approached the reception desk.

"Anne!"

The crisp British voice spun Anne around. Her eyes widened in shock as she saw Paula Wentworth rise from a table in a kiosk area adjacent to reception. Yet even as she recognised the other woman, shock faded into acceptance. It was not really surprising that Paula was here for Thady. Paula, walking smartly towards her, ready to protect Thady's interests.

She wore a black suit. Anne wondered if her clothes were terribly wrong. Perhaps it had been crazy to wear green, yet green was for spring, and hadn't Thady always associated her with spring? She had wanted to suggest to him that his long cold winter was over . . . if he chose it to be.

"What are you doing here?" Paula demanded, almost hissing the words at Anne as she reached her side.

"Thady's wife...she hasn't come out of the coma?" Anne asked, leaping straight to the most critical issue.

Paula shook her head. "There was never any real chance of that," she said impatiently.

"I'm neither selfish nor cruel, Paula," Anne burst out. "I didn't understand what Thady was telling me. I thought his wife was divorcing him and he didn't want to let her go. I had no idea of what was really happening until I forced Alex Korbett to tell me."

"Dear God!" Paula ran a shaky hand over her brow, then dropped it to clasp Anne's hand. Her eyes were grey with fatigue. "I came because I thought he needed someone. But you, Anne... Didn't he ask you to wait?"

"But I said I wouldn't. Don't you see?" she pleaded. "I can't let him think he's lost everyone, Paula. He has to know that there is a future with me and his son. If he wants it."

"I could tell him after it's over," Paula suggested, clearly doubtful about Anne's presence on the scene.

"Don't you think Thady might need to hear it from me? Wouldn't it save him pain if I told him now?" The agony of Anne's decision was in her strained voice.

"I don't know. I doubt if even Thady would know. I can't advise you on this, Anne."

"I don't know, either. But I swear to you I'm only thinking of Thady. It's not for me. Only for him, Paula."

Paula dragged in a deep breath. "Then you must do what you think is best."

"I've thought and thought about it. It's the only way I can see. I have to go to him."

Paula squeezed her hand sympathetically. "Has all this come about because of the words I said to you?"

Tears filmed Anne's eyes. "Yes. It was a turning point. I knew there had to be more that I didn't know. But really, it should never have been necessary. When you love someone, truly love someone, there's no room for secrets. This should have all come out a long time ago."

"I'll pray for both of you," Paula said huskily.

"Where do I go?"

"I'll walk with you to the door."

Anne struggled to regain composure as Paula steered her to an elevator. Once they had reached the right floor, Paula quietly indicated a sitting room where she would wait while Anne was with Thady. Then they walked along a wide corridor to the room at the end of it.

"Do you know what you're going to say?" Paula whispered, gesturing towards the closed door.

"I think so." The words trembled from Anne's lips. Her heart seemed to be slamming against her chest. "I feel terribly frightened."

"I'm frightened, too." Paula gave her shoulder a light squeeze. "Good luck, Anne."

"Thank you."

As Paula moved off down the corridor, Anne closed her eyes, took a deep breath and gathered her courage to the sticking point. This was right. It had to be.

She opened the door, stepped into the room, every nerve in her body wire-taut. It was a severely stark place, all white except for the banks of monitors grouped around the bed and attached in some fashion to the woman who lay there. Thady sat on the other side of her, his elbows on the bed, one of his wife's hands clasped between his and pressed to his lips. His eyes were closed, his head bowed as though in deep prayer.

Anne's resolution wavered. It seemed like sacrilege to break into such intense concentration. She glanced nervously at the woman Thady had loved and married, and her heart sank at the pure beauty of her face, a young, seemingly unmarked face, its smooth perfection framed by soft, red-gold curls.

Anne wrenched her gaze away, painfully conscious now of the dream that haunted Thady. It was not the past that had brought her here, she reminded herself. It was the future.

Yet the past lived in this room, Anne suddenly realised. At the foot of the bed was propped a framed photograph, Thady with his bride, a bride with a glorious wild halo of red-gold hair. In front of it lay a red rose, its rich scent dispelling the antiseptic atmosphere of the room.

Anne did not look any further. She did not want to see other mementos. They would make her feel even more of an intruder.

She quietly closed the door behind her, then forced herself to walk around the bed to where Thady was sitting. He did not stir. There was not the slightest reaction to anyone having entered the room. His absorption with his inner world was utterly complete.

Anne stood beside him, not daring to force her presence into this deep and private grief. After long silent, torturous minutes, she decided she couldn't. Her decision had been wrong. There had to be some other way to the future.

Tears blinded her eyes as she stepped back and turned. She carefully skirted the end of the bed, terrified of making any noise to draw attention to herself. She had to leave fast, yet she couldn't afford to hurry.

"Anne!"

The harsh rasp of her name froze her in mid-step. Panic churned through her as she darted a frantic look at Thady. His head was up. He had half risen from his chair, shock adding its ravages to the haggard lines of his face.

"I'm sorry. I'm sorry." The words spilled from her lips in a desperate rush. Tears raced uncontrollably down her cheeks.

"Why are you here?"

"So you wouldn't be alone. In case you needed me. To retract the terrible words I said to you in London when I didn't know what was happening. To help you in any way I can. To show you that your pain is my pain, Thady."

"No," he groaned. "I never meant to give you pain."

"There is no life without pain, Thady. Or love. I wanted you to know that all I have is yours to have. Or any part of it you choose. If you want it. Because I love you. Because I always will love you."

Thady sucked in a deep breath, but his face was impassive. A flicker of movement seemed to catch Anne's eye. She turned her head quickly, looked once more upon the figure in the bed and the bank of monitors. She was wrong. Nothing had moved. Nothing had changed.

"There's a waiting room just down the corridor," she said, her voice shaking with her inner misery. "I'll be there with Paula. If there's anything you want or need . . ." She shot one last pleading look at Thady.

His gaze was fastened on his wife's face. "Pray for her, if you will." His voice was strangely gentle.

"I will," she whispered, her voice choked with emotion.

She left as quickly and as quietly as she could. Paula looked inquiringly at her as she entered the waiting room. Anne sank gratefully into the armchair next to her.

"Bad?" Paula asked softly.

Tears swam into Anne's eyes again. "I failed. I should have respected his wishes. I should never have come. But I did learn something. Something very beautiful. I saw the pure face of love. The total giving of one person to another."

"Yes, I know," Paula murmured. "It's at the heart of his plays, isn't it?"

They lapsed into silence. Anne grieved over the thought that she could never take the place of Thady's wife. Then she found herself offering up a prayer for her. And another. And another.

Time dragged so slowly, the seconds seeming like minutes, the minutes like hours. A middle-aged couple walked past. They were sombrely dressed. The man's face was drawn with pained resignation. The woman was softly weeping.

"Her parents," Paula murmured discreetly.

Anne's thoughts returned to what was about to happen in the room at the end of the corridor, the pain and distress Thady must be feeling. She couldn't bear to look at her watch. She didn't want to know the exact moment of life giving way to death. She prayed a half-remembered litany for the dying.

The sound of sobbing broke the awful silence. The parents walked by again, heading back the way they had come, their heads bowed, the husband trying desperately to comfort his wife through his own tears of grief.

It had been done, Anne thought numbly, and nothing now could undo it. She wondered if the pain they had sought to end would ever be ended for them or for Thady. A blessed release, Paula had called it. But was it truly a release?

Anne stood up. She didn't want to be sitting down when Thady finally took his leave of the woman he had loved so much. She didn't know if he would come to the waiting room or pass by, as wrapped in grief as his parents-in-law had been. Paula stood beside Anne, silently lending her support. They waited, conscious of every second that passed. Finally there was the sound of slow footsteps in the corridor.

Thady appeared in the open doorway. His lips were bloodless, his face a ghastly grey. "It's over," he said, his voice as brittle as glass scraping over gravel.

Words were clearly inadequate. There was nothing that Anne could think of that would be adequate. She tried to show the sorrow she felt through her eyes.

Paula choked and took a half-step forward, her arms out-raised. Thady moved to meet her, wrapping her in a tight hug. "Thank you, old friend," he said gruffly. "It was good of you to come, but there's nothing you can do for me."

"Take care, Thady," Paula begged. After a brief pause, she looked up and fervently added, "We all need you." Then she returned his hug and said, "If you don't want anything from me, I'll go now."

"You can do me a favour, if you would."

"Anything at all."

"Look after Anne for me."

"I'll do everything I can."

"I'm sure you will."

Anne could feel the blood draining from her face at the implication of that requested favour. Thady was not coming back to her.

Thady released Paula and turned towards Anne. He made no move to draw her into an embrace. He took her two hands and placed them over his heart. Anne bravely lifted her chin to face whatever had to be faced. There was a pained plea for understanding in his eyes.

"I have to be alone, Anne."

"Of course," she agreed, biting her lip to hold back the tears.

"I need to come to terms with what has happened . . . with many things. I've got to start afresh. When I find the words I want to say, I'll write to you."

"I'll wait for that."

"Have you named our son?"

"Yes. Michael John."

"It's a beautiful name."

"I think so."

"You are beautiful, too." He bent his head and brushed his lips over hers in the gentlest of kisses, warm, tender, kind, but without the slightest shred of desire.

He drew back, released her hands, turned away.

"Thady . . ."

He paused, glanced back reluctantly.

Anne flushed, ashamed of wanting more than he could give right now. "How long do you think it might be?"

The weary hopelessness on his face was answer enough. "I don't know, Anne. I truly don't know. But I won't keep you waiting any longer than is absolutely necessary. When I can resolve it all in my mind and my heart, then you'll know."

He had said all he was going to say. Anne asked for no more. She stood there transfixed by a dread feeling of inevitability as she watched him go, each step away from her taking him on his solitary journey.

Paula moved to her side and curled her arm around Anne's. "New mothers need to be looked after," she said with caring kindness. "I promised Thady to look after you. I'm taking you home."

CHAPTER NINETEEN

IT WAS NEARLY three months before Anne heard from Thady. Although he had been perpetually on her mind, Anne had found a calm resignation within herself to carry her through whatever time Thady needed to come to a decision. Besides, she had Michael John to keep her busy and give her joy.

Jenny had long since gone home to Brian. Anne wrote to her regularly, giving news of the baby. Alex Korbett had appointed himself an honorary uncle and often visited them or took them out to some special event. Anne had become close friends with Paula Wentworth, who was always on hand to ensure Anne was well looked after. Taking everything into consideration, the three months had not been bad at all.

Until the parcel arrived in the mail from Thady.

A parcel, not a letter.

Anne stared at the postmark. It had been sent from Ireland, not America. Paula had told her he had family in Ireland. An elderly mother who refused to move from her home. A few cousins.

Anne opened the parcel with acute trepidation. The thick wad of pages bound in rubber bands had to be a manuscript. A new play. It was the first time, since she and Thady had come together, that he had written anything. There was a note attached to the front page.

Dear Anne,

I'm sorry it took so long to write this. I had great difficulty finding the words. There was so much to express. I hope you'll understand everything when you read it. I'll be with you and Michael John tomorrow.

Thady.

Anne lifted the note. The title of the play leapt up at her—*The Last Grand Passion*. Instantly a coil of revulsion tightened around her heart. She didn't want to read it. She had no doubt that it revolved around Thady's love for his wife and the loneliness and despair and grief that he had felt after her death.

Anne had lived through that. The last thing she wanted was to experience it again through Thady's play. Writing it all down might represent some kind of catharsis for him, but Anne was quite certain it could only give her more haunting memories of what he had felt for his wife. She wanted the past over. She wanted the future to begin.

Tomorrow, she thought, with a burgeoning of wild hope. Thady would be with her and Michael John tomorrow. Somehow, one way or another, Anne resolved to keep Thady with them. For the future.

She took the manuscript into his study and laid it on his desk. Then she went to the room she had turned into a nursery and smiled down at her baby, still sleeping peacefully from his mid-morning bottle. He was so beautiful. No way in the world could Thady resist loving him.

Later on in the afternoon, she took Michael John shopping and bought new outfits for both of them, a gorgeous red playsuit for Thady's son and a dark brown velvet pants-suit for herself.

Anne found it impossible to sleep that night. Her mind was full of nervous anticipation. Apart from which, she could not keep Thady's play out of her thoughts. He expected her to read it. He wanted her to know all he had thought and felt. She kept remembering her own words. *When you love someone, truly love someone, there's no room for secrets.*

Sharing was what love was all about. Sharing the good and the bad. *Your pain is my pain,* she had told him, and if she didn't live up to that, what would Thady think of her tomorrow? No matter how much pain it gave her, Anne decided, she had to read what Thady had written.

She pushed herself out of bed, went to his study and settled herself in the leather chair behind the desk, determined to read every word of Thady's play. Her hands trembled a little as she removed the rubber bands and lifted the title page aside.

The opening scene horrified her. There could be no doubt that *she* was Joanna, receiving a telephone call from the man she had loved seven years before. The words held her mesmerised, compelling her to read on and on, the complex passion between the two main characters reflecting so closely what had happened between her and Thady. *Her.* Not his wife.

It revealed many dimensions of feeling on Thady's side, the deep conflicts that had raged through him, the enormous swings from joy to despair and back again. It evoked memories that Anne had put aside, his horror at the thought that she might have some terrible medical problem that would rob him of her as he had been robbed of his wife. So many things gathered poignant meaning.

Anne wept and smiled in turn as his love for her took so many turnings. And always the passion, growing and deepening through every scene, winding around them, pulling them apart. Thady's words evoked every nuance of every emotion. Anne read to the last line, then sat there transfixed.

It was brilliant. More absorbing and compelling than *The Long Cold Winter*. Nothing Thady had ever written matched the grand sweep of this perception of the human heart. Yet the play was unfinished, the ending unresolved.

Anne felt it could go either of two ways. It could finish with the dark, stark tragedy that was Thady's hallmark. But for the first time in his life, he had written a glimmering of hope, a yearning for happiness, a tentative promise that this last grand passion would be fulfilled.

Tomorrow, Anne thought, her heart pumping its urgent hope for the ending she wanted. And surely Thady wanted it, too. Surely he did, or he would not be coming.

She could not believe he had written this play to commercialise what they had felt for each other. He had written it solely for her, to share with her, to banish forever the loneliness of secrets. It was an invitation to join her life with his, indissolubly, forever. That was what Thady had wanted her to understand before he came.

Anne hugged herself tightly as she realised her dreams might come true. All her dreams. She took herself to bed, willing tomorrow to come quickly, not wanting the dreams of yesterday but the reality that Thady would bring with him.

She was up early. She fed Michael John and dressed him in his new playsuit. She left him playing happily with an assortment of baby toys while she dressed herself for Thady, eager to look as beautiful as he thought her.

She had only just finished fussing over her appearance when she heard a knock at the front door. She raced to answer it. The door was already opening as she reached the living room. It had to be Thady, using his key.

He stepped into the room.

His arms opened to her as she flung herself against him. "You're home," she cried, her eyes sparkling with golden happiness as she looked up at his beloved face.

"Yes. I'm home at last," he said, his voice throbbing with the deep warmth of his happiness that it should be so.

He looked good. He felt good. Anne breathed a contented sigh. Thady had not come back to her for any healing this time. He had healed himself and had come to her a whole man, no longer torn apart by anything.

"Did you read the play?" he asked softly, his green eyes searching hers with hope and love.

"Yes. But it's not finished, Thady," she answered, her eyes mirroring the same feelings.

"That's for you to write, Anne. Any way you want."

"You tell me, Thady. What you've written is brilliant. The greatest play I've ever read. Only you can write the ending."

"It's not to be produced, Anne. Not unless you want it to be. It's my gift of love to you."

"Love in a play is one thing, Thady," she said a little sadly. "But I know the reality. I saw it between you and your wife."

He withdrew his arms to take her hands in his. He pressed a warm kiss in each palm then pressed them to his heart. His eyes were darkly serious as he answered her deepest concern, the memory that still had the power to haunt their future.

"Anne, the reason I was away so long was not just to write the play. I doubt that you'll believe what I have to tell you, but it's not the product of a distraught mind or a fevered imagination. It's a certainty that came with cool and calm reflection. Until I understood what it meant, only then could I be at peace with what I felt."

Anne's breath caught in her throat. This was what he had held back from the play, his last secret. This was the final moment of truth for her, the resolution that could go either way. "Go on," she pressed.

"You remember when you came to the hospital."

Anne nodded, not trusting herself to speak calmly about those traumatic moments.

"Just before you left, I asked you to pray for her...."

"I did, Thady. I did," Anne assured him solemnly.

"I was looking directly at my wife then. She smiled her approval at you, Anne."

"Not at me, Thady. Surely at you."

He shook his head. "It was just after you spoke of loving me."

A queer little shiver ran down Anne's spine. She remembered. Had she imagined movement, or had it been what Thady said it was?

"Afterwards, I had the monitors checked again and again and again. They all registered the same thing. Nothing happened. Yet, to my dying day, I'll swear she smiled at you."

"No. No, Thady." That couldn't be right, Anne reasoned to herself. Why would his wife smile at her? "I thought I saw it, too," she offered tentatively. "But when I looked there was nothing. Yet if she did smile, Thady, I'm sure it was at you."

"You saw it, too?"

Anne frowned over the memory, trying to recapture it. "There was something. It caught my eye. Then I thought I had to be wrong."

"The monitors registered no change. Not the slightest deviation. Yet I'm certain in my mind that I didn't imagine it."

"Then you didn't," Anne softly agreed.

He lifted a hand to her face, lightly stroking her cheek as though she was infinitely precious to him.

"For ten years I tried to reach her. If you hadn't come that day, if you hadn't said what you did, Anne, I would have been left with nothing. I think somehow she knew." He paused, his eyes roving slowly, adoringly over her features.

"What do you think she knew, Thady?" Anne prompted, needing to know what it meant to him.

"I've thought about it every day since then. I'm certain I know now. For the first time in all those years, she felt at peace, knowing that my life could go on, that I should share with you what I had once shared with her, that I should have my children with you and they'd be brought up with all the happy security of a love that lives through anything... anything at all."

His voice dropped to a low throb. "When we first met, Anne, you were like her in so many ways. You are now. I tried to keep you separate. Yet in some ways you are inseparable. In both nature and character. Fiercely independent. But generous in giving love and compassion. Braver than any man. Intensely loyal. Always committed to doing your best. Giving your utmost to what you believe in."

He drew her into his embrace again, and the look on his face was the look Anne had seen there once before and thought she would never see again. But it was there for her, and he said the words she had yearned to hear for so long.

"I love you, Anne. I always did. The difference now is that you have all my love. And I can, at long last, ask you to marry me. Will you be my wife?"

Her smile was illuminated by the unshadowed fulfilment of all she had ever wanted. "Yes, Thady. I want very much to be your wife, and for us to share the rest of our lives together."

His smile mirrored hers. "May I suggest we set the wedding date for the first day of spring?"

"What a lovely idea!"

"I promise I'll never leave you again, Anne. The rest of our lives we *will* be together. In everything."

Then he kissed her with all the passion Anne had been waiting for. A grand, wonderful passion, so deep it would last a lifetime.

A high-pitched shriek from the nursery broke into their absorption with each other. "The joys of parenthood." Anne laughed. Her eyes twinkled with happy teasing. "I believe that's your son calling for you, Thady."

"Mmm... Has quite an extraordinary voice box, hasn't he?"

"That is the sound of frustration. He has undoubtedly thrown his favourite toy out of the bassinette by accident and he wants you to hand it back to him."

Thady's laugh was a ripple of delight. His eyes sparkled with joyful anticipation as he hugged Anne to his side and set off to meet his son's needs.

His arms and legs were punching the air with furious energy, and his little face was screwed up ready to produce another yell when the faces of his mother and father suddenly hovered above him. This most satisfactory situation brought about a change of mind. He unscrewed his face, widened his eyes in limpid innocence and blew bubbles.

"You little rascal." Thady chuckled, hoisting the baby out of the bassinette and giving him all the indulgent attention that Michael John had been waiting for from his father.

The bonding between them was instant and complete, ratified by approving gurgles, absolutely absurd baby talk from a highly literate man and the possessive claim of tightly curled tiny fingers around a gently tickling thumb.

THE FIRST OF SPRING was a glorious day. In a little church on the outskirts of the village closest to Anne and Thady's new home in the country, Annelise Tolliver and Thady Riordan were married.

Alex Korbett gave the bride away.

Paula and Richard Wentworth served as matron of honour and best man.

All three sisters of the bride were present, accompanied by their husbands. Thady had flown the entire family to England for the occasion. Jenny's new baby daughter was being minded by Brian's parents in Australia, but she had dozens of photographs to match against Michael John, who watched the whole proceedings from the lap of his Australian grandmother.

Leonie Tolliver wept with sentimental joy as her oldest daughter walked triumphantly from the altar, a married woman at last. And what a photograph it would make to take pride of place on her mantelpiece! Not only did Anne look as beautiful as every bride should look, but on her earlobes glittered the most fabulous diamond earrings. They were a perfect match for Anne's engagement ring, which had been made by De Mestres in Brussels.

Of course, the wedding ring was the most important. But those diamonds would certainly show up in any photograph and demonstrate to all of Leonie's friends what a wonderfully generous man Anne had married. Handsome, famous, rich and generous. Really, when Anne finally set her mind on something, she certainly excelled. Even with marriage.

As the bride and groom posed on the front steps of the church to oblige the photographer, Thady smiled at his new wife and gently touched the diamond earrings that Anne was wearing for the first time in public. His eyes danced with pleasure.

"I take it this is a special occasion," he murmured.

"They feel right on me today," Anne replied, her face radiant with love for him.

"Everything is right today," Thady declared.

Without any prompting from the photographer, Thady Riordan took his wife in his arms and kissed her with all the passionate rightness he felt, and Annelise Riordan responded in the same way.

Everybody there could see how deeply in love they were. Michael John Patrick Riordan celebrated the moment by reciting the two words he had learnt, "Dada" and "Muma." Then he pulled off his shoes and played with his toes. He laughed and he gurgled and he burbled. He knew with absolute certainty that not only was everything right today, but everything would be right forever more.

POSTSCRIPT

Thady Riordan went on to write some of the most magical plays to ever touch the human heart. Annelise Riordan did the production design for all of them. *The Last Grand Passion* was never produced.

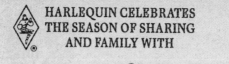

HARLEQUIN CELEBRATES
THE SEASON OF SHARING
AND FAMILY WITH

Harlequin introduces the latest member in its family of
seasonal collections. Following in the footsteps of the popular
My Valentine, Just Married and *Harlequin Historical Christmas
Stories*, we are proud to present FRIENDS, FAMILIES,
LOVERS. A collection of three new contemporary romance
stories about America at its best, about welcoming others into
the circle of love.... Stories to warm your heart...

By three leading romance authors:

> ### KATHLEEN EAGLE
> ### SANDRA KITT
> ### RUTH JEAN DALE

Available in October, wherever
Harlequin books are sold.

1993 Keepsake

CHRISTMAS

Stories

Capture the spirit and romance of Christmas with KEEPSAKE CHRISTMAS STORIES, a collection of three stories by favorite historical authors. The perfect Christmas gift!

Don't miss these heartwarming stories, available in November wherever Harlequin books are sold:

ONCE UPON A CHRISTMAS by Curtiss Ann Matlock
A FAIRYTALE SEASON by Marianne Willman
TIDINGS OF JOY by Victoria Pade

ADD A TOUCH OF ROMANCE TO YOUR HOLIDAY SEASON WITH KEEPSAKE CHRISTMAS STORIES!

HX93